I0778398

George A. Taylor

The Sequel

Outlook

George A. Taylor

The Sequel

1. Auflage | ISBN: 978-3-73262-697-7

Erscheinungsort: Frankfurt am Main, Deutschland

Erscheinungsjahr: 2018

Outlook Verlag GmbH, Frankfurt.

Reproduction of the original.

George A. Taylor

The Sequel

Outlook

THE SEQUEL

WHAT THE GREAT WAR WILL MEAN TO AUSTRALIA.

Being the Narrative of "Lieutenant Jefson, Aviator."

By

GEORGE A. TAYLOR.

First Edition, June. 1915.
2nd Edition. July. 1915.

Printed and Published by Building Limited.
17 Grosvenor Street. Sydney,
Australia.

BY THE SAME AUTHOR.

1910.—"The Air Age and its Military Significance."

1911.—"The Highway of the Air and the Military Engineer."

1913.—"The Balkan Battles." How Bad Roads Lost a War.

1913.—"The Schemers." (A Story.)

1913.—"Songs for Soldiers." 1914.—

"Town Planning for Australia."

"Ah! when Death's hand our own warm hand hath ta'en
  Down the dark aisles his sceptre rules supreme,
God grant the fighters leave to fight again
  And let the dreamers dream!"
—Ogilvie.

PREFACE

These are mighty days.

We stand at the close of a century of dazzling achievement; a century that gave the world railways, steam navigation, electric telegraphs, telephones, gas and electric light, photography, the phonograph, the X-ray, spectrum analysis, anæsthetics, antiseptics, radium, the cinematograph, the automobile, wireless telegraphy, the submarine and the aeroplane!

Yet as that brilliant century closed, the world crashed into a war to preserve that high level of human development from being dragged back to barbarism.

And how the scenes of battle change!

Cities are being smashed and ships are being torpedoed. Thousands of lives go out in a moment. And these tremendous tragedies pass so swiftly that it is risky to write a story round them carrying any touch of prophecy. I, therefore, attempt it, realising that risk. The story is written for the close of the year 1917. Its incidents are built upon the outlook at June, 1915.

It first appeared in an Australian weekly journal, "Construction," in January, 1915, and already some of its early predictions have been realised; as, for instance, the entry of Italy in June, the use of "thermit" shells, and the investigation of "scientific management in Australian work."

To many readers, some of the predictions may not pleasantly appeal. But it must be remembered that, being merely predictions, they are not incapable of being made pleasant in the practical sense. In other words, should any threaten to develop truth, to materialise, all efforts can be concentrated in shaping them to the desired end.

Predictions are oftentimes warnings. Many of these are.

The story is written to impress the people, with their great responsibilities in these wonderful days—when a century of incident is crowded into a month, when an hour contains sixty minutes of tremendous possibilities, when each of us should live the minutes, hours, days and weeks with every fibre strained to give the best that is in us to help in the present stupendous struggle for the defence of civilisation.

GEORGE A.
TAYLOR.

Sydney, Australia, June, 1915.

The map, on pages 6 and 7, shows the lines followed by the German armies through Belgium and France during August and September, 1914. The main line of the Allies' attack, through Metz, in August and September, 1915, culminating in the defeat of Germany (predicted for the purpose of this story) is also shown.

You can facilitate the early realisation of this prediction by enlisting NOW.

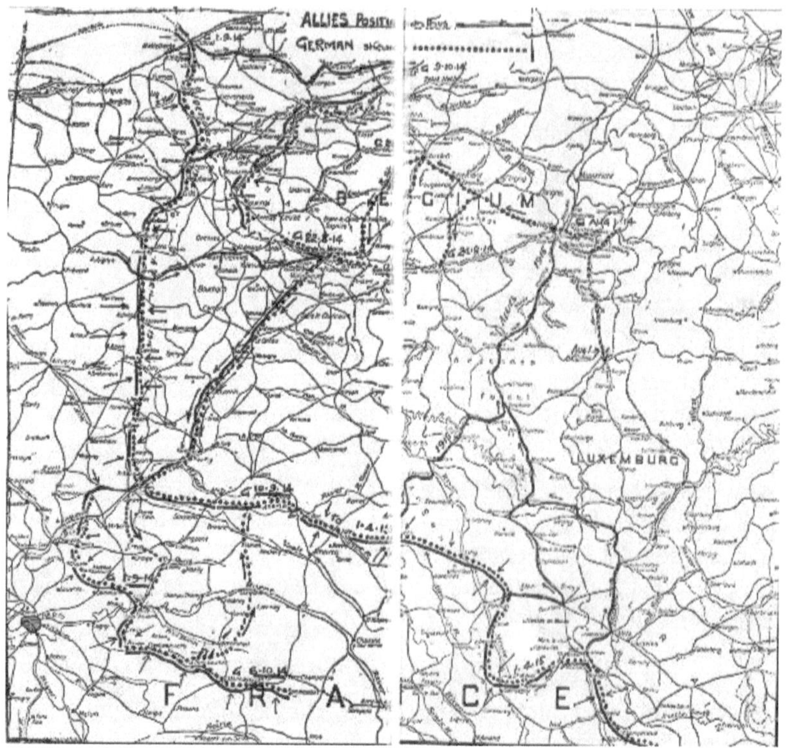

They often met before and fought.
To gain supremacy in sport.
They meet again now side by side.
For freedom in the whole world wide.

CHAPTER I.

Winged!

It was the second day in February, 1915.

I'll not forget it in a hurry. That day I fell into the hands of the German Army. "Fell," in my case, was the correct word, for my monoplane was greeted with a volley of shots from some tree-hidden German troops as I was passing over the north-eastern edge of the Argonne Forest.

I was returning from Saarbruck when I got winged. Bullets whizzed through the 'plane, and one or two impinged on the engine. I tried to turn and fly out of range, but a shot had put the rudder out of action. An attempt to rise and trust to luck was baulked by my engine losing speed. A bullet had opened the water cooler, and down, down the 'plane glided, till a clear space beyond a clump of trees received it rather easily. I let the petrol run out and fired it to put the machine out of use. Then a rifle cracked and a bullet tore a hole through my left side, putting me into the hospital for six weeks.

That forced idleness gave me plenty of time for retrospection.

I lived the previous energetic five months over and over again. I had little time before to think of anything but my job and its best possibilities, but the quietness of the hospital at Aix la Chapelle made the previous period of activity seem a nightmare of incident.

I remember how surprise held me that I should be lying wounded in a German hospital—I, a lieutenant in the Royal Flying Corps, who for years before the war, had actually been a member of an Australian Peace Society!

Zangwill's couplet had been to me a phrase of force:—

> "To safeguard peace—we must prepare for war.
> I know that maxim—it was forged in Hell!"

I remembered well how I had hung on the lips of Peace Advocate Doctor Starr Jordan during his Australian visits, and how I had wondered at his stories that Krupp's, Vicker's, and other great gun-building concerns were financially operated by political, war-hatching syndicates; that the curse of militarism was throttling human progression, and that the doctrine of "non- resistance" was noble and Christianlike, for "all they that take the sword shall perish by the sword."

I remembered how in Australia I had grieved that aviation, in which I took a keen interest as a member of the Aerial League, was being fostered for military purposes instead of for that glorious epoch foretold by Tennyson:—

> For I dipped into the future far as human
> eye could see,
> Saw the vision of the world and all the
> wonders that would be,
> Saw the heavens filled with commerce,
> Argosies of magic sails,
> Pilots of the purple twilight, dropping
> down with costly bales.

I remembered I felt that the calm of commerce held far more glories than the storm of war; that there was no nobler philosophy than:—

> "Ye have heard it said, an eye for an eye, and a tooth for a tooth; but I say … resist not evil; but whosoever shall smite thee on thy right cheek, turn to him the other also. If any man take thy coat, let him have thy cloke also."

Then came the thunderclap of war; and in the lightning flash I saw the folly of the advocacy of peace. I felt that I, like others, had held back preparation for this great war, that had been foreseen by trained minds. I felt that extra graves would have to be dug, because dreamers—like myself—had prated peace instead of helping to make our nation more secure.

"Non-resistance" may be holy, but it encourages tyranny and makes easy the way of the wrongdoer. If every man gave his cloak to the thief who stole his coat, there would be no inducement for the robber to lead an honest life. Vice would be more profitable than virtue.

"Non-resistance" may be saintly, but it would make it impossible to help the weak or protect the helpless from cruelty and outrage.

All law, all justice, rests on authority and force. A judge could not inflict a penalty unless there were force to carry it out.

Creeds, after all, are tried in the fires of necessity. "They that take the sword shall perish by the sword." Well, the Kaiser had grasped the sword. By whose sword should he perish except by that of the defender?

Christ's teachings are characterised by sanity and strength. He speaks of His angels as ready to fight for Him; He flogged the moneychangers from the temple: He said that no greater love can be shown than by a man's laying down his life for his friend; and the Allies fighting bravely to protect the oppressed, were manifesting to the full this great love. Germany's attack on a weaker nation, which she had signed to protect, called for punishment from other nations who had also pledged their honor.

Unhappy Belgium called to the civilised world to check the German outrages on its territory and people.

My peace doctrines went out like straw before a flame. I was a "peace-dove" winged by grim circumstance; and that is how I became a man of war.

HOW HISTORY REPEATED ITSELF.
England to Belgium, in 1870: "Let us hope they (Germany) will not trouble you, but if they do—"
(Tenniel, in "London Punch," at the time of the Franco-Prussian War.)

CHAPTER II.

The First Three Months of War.

I was in England when the war cloud burst, having just completed a course of aviation at the Bristol Flying Grounds; so I volunteered for active service; and, after a month's military training, was appointed a lieutenant in Number 4 Squadron of the R.F.C.

I remember how the first crash of war struck Europe like a smash in the face. How armies were rapidly mobilised! How the British Fleet steamed out into the unknown, and Force became the only guarantee of national safety!

It is hard to write of these things now that many days have passed between, for events followed each other with the swiftness of a mighty avalanche.

How Germany thrilled the universe by throwing at Belgium the greatest army the world had ever seen. An awful wave of 1,250,000 men crashed upon the gate of Liege.

How the great Krupp siege guns slowly crawled up, stood out of range of the Liege forts, and broke them at ease.

How through the battered gate a flood of Uhlans poured to make up for that wasted fortnight, preceded by their Taube aeroplanes spying out the movements of the Belgium army; the German artillery following, and smashing a track through France!

How that fortnight gave France and England the chance to interpose a wall of men and steel, which met the shock of battle at Mons, but was pushed back almost to the gates of Paris.

It was at the battle of Mons that the squadron to which I was attached went into active operation, reconnoitring the battle line on our left flank. It was my first taste of battle, but I do not remember any strange feelings.

I was in that awful shock of forces that stopped the southern progress of the German juggernaut like a chock beneath a wheel, when on September 2 it recoiled back—back to the Marne—back to the Aisne—back almost to the Belgian frontier. Then winter dropped upon it, turning the roads into pools of mud, checking all speed movements necessary to active operations, and the troops dug in like soldier crabs upon a river bank.

"The Aeroplane had been a ... curiosity."—Chapter III.
(The first Aeroplane to fly in Australia.)

All surprise movements had to be made at night; the dawn finding our aeroplanes out in the frosty air spying out any changes in positions of the day before. A smoke-ball fired as we flew above a new trench gave our artillery the range; then till night fell a rain of shells would batter that new position. In the dark our troops would creep forward, rush that trench, and dawn would find them dozing in their newly won quarters. The war had become a battle of entrenchments.

CHAPTER III.

The Flying Men.

For ages man walked the earth.

To-day he is the only living creature that can travel in the air by other than its own substance.

'Till the Great War the aeroplane was a scientific curiosity. The Battle of the Nations blooded it; and its wonderful utility in speeding the end of the war has proved its right to be recognised as a distinct factor in human movement.

When the war crash came there were two aerial types; the lighter than air type, the dirigible balloon; and the heavier than air machine, the aeroplane. This is how the Powers stood in aerial furnishing when the first shot was fired. Germany and Austria had 25 airships, including 11 Zeppelins, as well as 556 aeroplanes.

England, France, Russia and Belgium had 33 airships and 1019 aeroplanes.

The English dirigibles had not made long flights, and not being very dependable had not received much attention from the military authorities. A non-dependable factor in war is worse than useless. A mistake may be made in tactics, but when ascertained may be retrieved and, perhaps, turned to good account. Non-dependability is fatal, as many a commander would not know how to act, and in war, he who hesitates is lost.

The French had experimented a good deal with the dirigible, but mostly of the non-rigid type, which was a type "without a backbone" and was as uncertain, so that its general non-dependability turned French attention to the aeroplane.

The Germans, however, pinned their faith on the balloon, and for long made it a feature for observation purposes, so that when Zeppelin brought out his rigid framework balloon, Germany fancied she saw in it the command of the air.

The Zeppelin, however, had many disabilities over the aeroplane. It had to have its own kennel. It was almost impossible to get it into its shed if the wind was against it. The kennels had, therefore, to be either on wheels or floating. Furthermore, not being able to replenish its gas, a Zeppelin had always to return to its base for supplies. But the gas balloon suited the smug character of the German. Unlike the aviator who threw himself into the air on a bundle of steel rods and rubber, a propeller and a petrol engine, the phlegmatic German took no risks with a balloon. He found, however, that Zeppelins were expensive freaks. They had a habit of catching fire in the air, because the tail created a vacuum and sucked back some escaping gas into the engine where the contact spark ignited it.

One recently alighted in a field and a country bumpkin came over with the crowd to see the fun. He had a pipe in his mouth. He was told to go away. He wouldn't for a while, but he soon left in a hurry. After the explosion they found bits of him and sixty-seven other people!

The Germans pinned their faith to the Zeppelin because it could carry a heavy load of explosives and would be an easy way of damaging an enemy; and it was only a few months before the war that considerable enthusiasm ruled Germany because a Zeppelin had made a record trip from the southern to the northern fringe of Germany, or, as "Vorwarts" said, "as far as from Germany to England and back again."

Here, then, was an easy way to fight. Just rise up out of danger and drop bombs.

They tried it at Antwerp.

On 25th August, 1915, a Zeppelin flew over the sleeping city, guided by flash lamps from German spies on roofs. It was a night of terror—a bomb dropped to fall upon the royal palace, missed and injured two women; a bomb aimed for the Antwerp Bank missed and killed a servant; but one fell into a hospital and another into a crowd in the city square. Five people were blown to atoms.

It must have been an awful night, for it is recorded that the city watchman of Antwerp announced: "12 o'clock and all's hell."

On September 2nd (the anniversary of Sedan), the Zeppelin came again to give its stab in the dark, but finding it was recognised, retreated. It did not rise higher to get out of danger of the air guns and put up a fight. The German in the air takes few risks. It is his temperament. Not so with the Frenchman. He is by nature dashing and volatile. The easy-going of the dirigible little appealed to him. The risk, the speed, the adventure of the aeroplane touched his soul, which explained why France had 2032 military aviators, whilst Germany had only 300 qualified military pilots.

The German lacks the dash, nerve, vim and initiative essential to a successful flier. He is moulded as a cog. He is part of a system—out of that he must not move. It has wrecked his initiative, and the sneer of the greatest German in history, Frederick the Great, has to-day grim significance.

"See those two mules," he said satirically to one of his officers, who lacked initiative, "they have been in fifteen campaigns and—they're still mules."

The German training system has taken all the humanity out of the men. They move like machines, either destroying or rolling on to destruction, and they often act with the dumb sense of the machine to pain and suffering.

Lloyd George has very truly put it: "God made man to his own image, but the German recreated him in the form of a Diesel engine."

No one questioned the efficiency of the German machine. The Allies were disputing its right to go on destroying.

"The New Arm."—Chapter IV.

CHAPTER IV.

The New Arm.

"It strikes me that these fool commanders don't know what to do with us. We aviators seem to be too new to come into all their stunts. Here we've been flying over eight years, and we're still novel enough to be repeatedly fired on by our own side. Why the beggars in our own battery, when they see an aeroplane overhead in their excitement let fly. They don't bother to notice that the plane of our Bleriot hasn't claw ends like the enemy's Taube. Neither do they note we carry our own distinguishing mark. We're the circus show. We're the 'comic relief' sure."

He was about to spit his disgust on an unoffending fly, but quickly changed his mind.

He was a Yank from the U.S.A. Military School at San Diego, and "hiked over the pond as there was nothing doing."

In appearance he was tall and wiry with a thin face and hooked nose that suggested the bird-man. His name on the roll was Walter Edmund Byrne, but his bony appearance won him his nickname—Nap.

We knew nicknames would shock those who stand for the rigid rule of military discipline, but aviators clear the usual wall of demarcation between officers and subordinates. A nod supplants the "heels together and touch your cap."

The Aviation Sections seemed to be communistic concerns, in the air rank being only recognised by achievement. In fact, the new arm was too new to be brought under the iron rule of military etiquette or into most Operation Orders. I told Nap as much.

"Yes," he said, "I guess we're too new. Even when cannon first came into war it was novel enough to fire as often from the wrong end and teach things 'to the man behind the gun'; but I've a bit of dope here that ought to be pasted into every book of your field service regulations, and every officer ought to repeat it before breakfast three times a week. It's the flyers' creed."

Fumbling amongst some newspaper scraps in his note book, he produced this bit of verse.

> The snake with poisoned fang defends
> (And does it really very well).
> The cuttle fish an inkcloud sends;

The tortoise has its fort of shell;
The tiger has its teeth and claws;
  The rhino has its horns and hide;
The shark has rows of saw-set jaws;
  Man—stands alone, the whole world
wide
Unarmed and naked! But 'tis plain
  For him to fight—God gave a brain!

Far back in this world's early mists
  When man began to use his head;
He stopped from fighting with his fists
  And gripped a wooden club instead.
But when the rival tribe was slain,
  The first tribe then to stand alone
Had once again to work its brain
  And made an axe—an axe of stone!
The stone-axe tribe would hold first
place;
  And ruled the rest where'er it went.
Because then—as to-day—the race
  Was first that had best armament.
But human brain expanding more
  (Its limits none can circumscribe);
The stone-axe crowd went down before
  The more developed bronze-axe tribe.
Then shields came in to quickly show
  Their party victors in the strife:
By warding off the vicious blow
  And giving warriors longer life.
The tribe's wise men would urge at
length,
  No doubt as now, for tax on tax,
To keep the "Two tribe" fighting
strength
  With "super-dreadnought" shield and
axe!

The bow and arrow came and won
  For Death came winged from far
away.
Then came the cannon and the gun;

> And brought us where we are to-day.
> And now we see the shield of yore
>   An arsenal of armour plate;
> With crew a thousand men or more;
>   And guns a hundred tons in weight.
> Beneath our seas dart submarines,
>   Around the world and back again.
> But every marvel only means
>   Some greater triumph of the brain.
> For while the thund'ring hammers ring;
>   And super-dreadnoughts swarm the
> sea;
> There flits above, a birdlike thing,
>   That claims an aerial sovereignty!
> A thing of canvas, stick and wheel
>   "The two-man fighting aeroplane."
> It screams above those hulks of steel:
>   "Oh! human brain begin again."

Nap was busy with bad language, a size brush and some fabric remnants patching the plane, whilst I read his treasure by my pocket lamp. Then he came over.

"Mind you," he said, "I don't greatly blame folks here. It can't be worse than in America—America, where the first machine got up and made good—

where the man the world had waited for for ages, Wilbur Wright (though he's been dead some years), hasn't even got a tablet up to say: 'Good on you old man, God rest your soul.'"

We were standing by our machines, waiting for the dawn light to call us aloft for our daily reconnaissance when Nap let his tongue loose.

"Five years ago, when the Wright Brothers first flew, Europe went dotty and began to offer big prizes for stunts in the air. Wright took his old 'bus across the pond and won everything. Next year our Glen Curtis went over and brought back all the scalps. Then America got tired. We live in a hurry there. We're the spoilt kids of the earth, always wanting a new toy. When we tired of straight flying, we went in for circus stunts; such as spiral turning, volplaning, upside-down flying and looping the loop. We interested the crowd for a while, as there was a chance of some of us smashing up. But when flying got safe and sane and the aeroplane almost foolproof, the public got cold feet, and the only men flying when I left, were young McCormick, the Harvester chap of Chicago, occasionally hiking across Lake Michigan in his 'amphoplane,' and Beechy, dodging death in 'aeroplane versus automobile' races.

"Curtis has a factory that had been shooing the bailiff till Wanamaker came along and financed that Atlantic aeroplane that was too heavy to carry its weight; and Lieutenant Porte, who was to take it across, was in a fix till this war came along and called him over. Orville Wright is trying to make a do of his factory. It is significant that Captain Mitchell, of the U.S. Signal Corps, the other day asked the U.S. Government 'to help those fellows out or they'll have to quit the business.' So you see Jefson, that's why I get the huff when I see the same sort of thing over here, especially in times like these 'that try men's souls.'"

Then the dawn light streaked the eastern sky rim. We pulled the plane from under the tree screen. The propeller hummed, dragged us across a dozen yards and up into the cold air of the early New Year morn.

"When flying got safe and sane."—Chapter IV.

CHAPTER V.

The Tired Feeling.

Our quarters were outside Epernay, about fifteen miles south of Rheims, with the Marne between us and the enemy.

To the north the horizon was fringed with the ridge-backed plateau cut by the Aisne. The enemy had been holding that fringe since October, having pushed back our almost daily attempts to get on to it. We got a particularly bad smack early in 1915, after crossing at Soissons.

To the north east was the ridge covered by the Argonne Forest; a sealed area to the man in the air.

We had been here three months, and our daily flight over the same area robbed the view of any scenic interest.

Perhaps, in the clear air of the winter morning, we would see far off silhouetted against the pale green of the brightening eastern sky, the dove-like aeroplanes of the enemy moving over the distant forest like bees above a bush.

Sometimes an "affair of aerial patrols" would result in the exchange of long shots, but seldom with any effect, for the reason that our enemy took few risks in the air and, furthermore, we could not pursue, as our orders were for speedy reconnaissance and early report. This was no easy matter over a country covered with the snowy quilt of winter, when even trees were unrecognisable, except at an angle that would show the trunks beneath: an angle that would call for low flying, bringing us within the 6000 feet range of the enemy's "air-squirts."

By day we "trimmed our ship," examined every screw and bolt and inspected our bombs and fuses. These "cough drops" were radish-shaped shells, each weighing thirty-one pounds; and were fired from an apparatus which could be worked by the pilot and which carried a regulator showing height and speed of the machine. Fair accuracy could thus be achieved.

One evening, the commander of the battery to which we were attached came over to our quarters, the skillion of a wrecked farm house.

He brought word that another Zeppelin had been rammed by one of our machines. Both machines and their occupants had been smashed.

He spoke in French, and we understood, which explained why we were stationed so far east on the fighting line.

"Magnificent it must have been," he said, "we groundlarks always have a fighting chance, but there is no chance for you bird-men. Ah! who can now say the romance has gone out of war with the improvement in range of weapons. Time was not long since when the general headed his men with a waving sword. As your Shakespeare said it—'Once more into the breach, dear friends.' And my comrades are fighting through this campaign, banging at an enemy they may never see. But the aeroplane has brought back the romance again. Ah! it is fine."

When he strolled out Nap ventured his opinion.

"Romance in war! There's not a scrap of it. The fool-flyer who rams a Zepp. deserves what he gets. It's wasteful for a flyer to so risk his speedy plane, when he has a better fighting chance of rising and dropping 'cough-drops' on the slow old 'bus beneath him; as Pegoud told us the other day: 'The Zeppelins! Ah, they are slow as geese, but our aeroplanes, they are swift as swallows.'

"The trouble is there's not enough opportunity here to do things. This daily 'good-morning fly' and cleaning engines the rest of the day is getting on my nerves, we've been marking time here for months. I want something to happen along 'right soon.'"

And something did happen along next morning.

CHAPTER VI.

Civilised Warfare.

Nap was in a bad humor.

The breeze from the north-east had kept us up for three days. It came to us over fields of long-unburied dead. It explained our morbid craving for tobacco—and Nap, during the night, had lost a cherished half-cigar!

We felt the cold that morning, as we wheeled the 'plane into the open space. The engine was also out of sorts, coughing like an asthmatic victim.

The first sun ray shot into the sky and called us aloft. So with engine spluttering the 'plane climbed over the Marne-Vesle Ridge and above the cloud of smoke that hid Rheims 5000 feet below us.

Looking far to the north-west, a great fog cloud lay over the wet country of the Yser. About twenty-five miles off, near Laon, we spotted one of the enemy's observation balloons being inflated.

"Shall we drop a 'cough-drop'?" Nap shouted to me through the speaking tube.

"No chance," I shouted back, "there's something coming at us."

A swift Taube was racing up to challenge. It was rising to get the "drop" on us. We carried an aerial gun, but hesitated to fire, as we wanted all our speed to get above our rival. Our engine lost its bad temper for a change. Round and round we began to circle like game cocks spoiling for a fight; rising, forgetting, in the excitement, the cold of the upper air—higher and higher, till Nap shouted, "We'll get her beneath us in the next round and then for a 'cough-drop' or the gun."

But the Taube had seen our advantage. It banked up on a sharp turn, dropped like a stone fully a thousand feet, making a magnificent volplane, and scurried away like a frightened vulture, dropping and dropping in a series of gigantic swoops.

"We won't chase," said Nap, "she wants to bring us into range of their 'air-squirts,' and 'Archibalds' are not pleasant on an empty stomach."

"ONE OF THE ENEMY'S 'AIR-SQUIRTS.'"
A German Aerial Gun.

We turned home and then the engine sulked again. I could see Nap was in trouble. It was was just as well that the roar of the engine and the hum of the propeller compelled the use of speaking-tube communication, for when a man uses bad language he isn't cool enough to pour his sentiments through a pipe. But we were coming down, gliding down on a long angle, with the engine giving a spasmodic kick. Down, down towards a light fog that the breeze had brought down from the north-west; down, down till we could see below us trench lines that were not our own! Then the engine stopped!

Nap looked out, turned to me and pulled a face. Putting his mouth to the tube he shouted "Lean over and wave your hand like...."

Several grey-coated soldiers were now running over to a bare patch to which we seemed to be sliding. I waved frantically—the soldiers hesitated to fire and waved back again! Down, down, with Nap working like a fiend at the engine! Down, down to within a few hundred feet of the ground, when something happened. The engine, after a splutter, set off at its usual rattle, the propeller caught up its momentum and descent was checked.

Nap leaned over and joined in the waving demonstration and, knowing that an attempt to rise abruptly would give away the fact that we were trying to escape, he kept at a low level, flying over waving Germans, past a long line of German troops breakfasting behind the trenches; then back again to try and convince them that we were of their own, then circling around till we reached a safe height above the thickening fog, our aching arms stopped waving. We headed for home, and repaid the kindness of our German friends by having their position shelled for the rest of the day.

"That was a tight fix," Nap ventured, as I gave him a tribute from the Squadron Commander—one of the most coveted of prizes of the campaign— a cigar!

"Yes, that waving stunt was a bit of spice," he said.

"But what beats me," I replied, "is why they didn't fire on us, as we carried our distinguishing mark."

"That's easy," said Nap, sucking his cigar, "they've got some of their own 'planes carrying our mark and guessed we were one of them. But as the song says: 'We're all here, so we're alright.' Some of these days I'm going to invent an apparatus that can change signs—press a button and the Germans' black cross will cover our mark, and so on—and then we'll fly where we like."

"It's unfair to fly an enemy's flag, you know, Nap," I ventured.

"How?" he queried. "That's where the Allies, particularly you hypersensitive British, make the greatest mistake. Everything in war is fair. Get the war over, say I, even if it comes to smashing up the enemy's hospitals. The wounded, nowadays, are getting well too quickly. There's a fellow in that battery yonder who has been in the hospital twice already, and, if this war lasts out Kitchener's tip of three years, practically the whole of the armies will have gone up for alterations and repairs, and be as lively as ever on the firing line. The Geneva Treaty, that prohibits firing on the Red Cross in time of war, is like any other 'scrap of paper.' I'd wipe out the enemy's hospitals and poison his food supplies. It's an uncivilised idea, I guess, but so is war. What's the difference between tearing out a fellow's 'innards' with a bayonet, and killing him by the gentler way of poisoning his liquor? What's the difference between poisoning the enemy's drinking water and poisoning the enemy's air with the new-fangled French explosive—Turpinite? It's all hot air talking of the enemy's barbarism—scratch the veneer off any of us and we're back into the stone age. If I had a free leg or free wing, I'd drop arsenic in every reservoir in Germany. Why, we're even prevented dropping 'coughs' on those long strings of trains we see every day, crawling far beyond the enemy's line carrying supplies from their bases to the firing line, feeding 'em up, feeding 'em up all the time."

We chafed at this restriction of our possibilities.

It gave Nap a fine opportunity for nasty remarks.

"Here we've got the most wonderful arm of the war, and the men over us don't know how to appreciate it. It's the same old prejudices, as my old

Colonel, Sam Reber, used to say, 'every new thing has to fight its way.' It's the same with wireless. Here they're only using it for tiddly widdly messages, like school kids practising with pickle bottles, when they could use it to guide a balloon loaded with explosives and fitted up with a wireless receiver and a charged cell, so that it could be exploded by a wave when it got over a position or a city. I'd like to see this fight a war of cute stunts, a battle of brains against brains, but I suppose we'll have to stick here till our fabrics rot whilst those fellows out yonder are burrowing into the earth like moles, coming out at night, like cave-men, and battling with a club."

CHAPTER VII.

What Australia was Doing.

That day I had a letter from Australia. Here it is:—

"Dear Jefson,—Your cheery letter from the front was full of the powder and shot of action and riotous optimism. I'm afraid mine will be a contrast.

"Our Australia isn't faring well. Our vigorous assertion of the strength of our young nationhood has been manifested only in a military and naval sense—commercially, we are nearly down and out.

"We are outrageously pessimistic. There was an excuse at the beginning of the war, when we dropped behind a rock, stunned at the very thought of an Armageddon; then we clapped our hands on our pockets, tightened up our purse strings, and, with white faces, waited for the worst and—we're still waiting. There was an excuse for us to be absolutely flabbergasted when the Kaiser's crowd rushed on to Paris. There may have been reason then for more than ordinary caution, but since the 'great check,' there has been no valid reason for people to still sit tight and wait. People with money to invest are holding up most of the former avenues of activity. 'Till the war is over' is the only excuse they can mumble.

"Take building investments in Sydney alone. A friend showed me a list of ninety-one plans held up, totalling over £4,000,000; held up 'till the war is over,' held up till the accumulated business will rush like an avalanche, running prices that are now low to such a high figure that the fools who waited will find they will have lost thousands. Building prices are now fifteen per cent. cheaper than before the war and twenty-five per cent. cheaper than they will be when the war has broken. Twenty-five per cent. means a distinct loss of £1,000,000 in one avenue of investment alone, not counting the tying up of the many hundreds other lines depending upon building construction— and when you consider, Jefson, that such inactivity is almost everywhere, you can guess we're in for a bad time if people don't buck up. To make matters worse, some firms are stopping advertising, forgetting that advertising is the life-blood of their business, and by stopping advertising they're stopping circulation of money. The firm that thinks it can save money by stopping advertising is in the same street as the man who thinks he can save time by stopping the clock.

"These are no ordinary firms, but what the local Labor League is so fond of describing as 'capitalistic institutions.' They hold many thousands in reserve and their annual dividends have been at least 10 per cent. for years and years and years. Moreover their businesses have not materially suffered. In some cases, indeed, there has been improvement. But 'profits' evidently supersede humanity; the interests of gold are greater than the welfare of human flesh and blood and even the call of country. It seems hard, Jefson, that you should be risking your life and other brave fellows shedding their blood, for such men who have neither commercial instinct nor human feeling. I fully expected some of those firms to start their jobs as an incentive to others. We only want someone to start and do something big to galvanise the smaller investors into action. It's not capital they lack, but confidence.

"I often wonder why the men who have had the acumen to amass money have not the common sense to realise that unemployed capital is a rapidly-accruing debt. Sovereigns by themselves are not wealth. It is their purchasing capacity and their equivalent in the requirements of life that represent fortunes. Investment, not idle capital, is wealth.

"Australia is being held back a great deal by the operation of State Enterprise. It has always been extravagant, inefficient and slow; but the effects are being more keenly felt at this time. At Cockatoo Island, the Federal Shipbuilding Yard, a cruiser was built that could not be launched. (I don't want you to mention this because we feel mighty humiliated.) Someone blundered. Who that someone was I do not suppose we shall ever know. That is the worst of being an employer of politicians. They run your business when they like, how they like, and with whom they like. You only come in on the pay day. However, the difficulty is being got over by the construction of a coffer-dam
—at a cost of £30,000. We have been confidently assured by the men running our business that everything will be all right in the long run. Perhaps that assurance is intended as a guarantee that we shall get a long run for our money. Anyhow, at time of writing the coffer-dam is being constructed.

"In N.S.W. the position of the Public Works Department must be much the same as the Sultan of Turkey's—no money, no friends. And no wonder! It drained the State of all spare cash for the edification of its day-labor joss, and is about to pawn the State to foreign money lenders for more. Being now on its absolute uppers, the Public Works Department is handing over work to a private syndicate to be carried out on a percentage basis. The longer the work takes and the more it costs, the better for the private company. Here again the public pays.

"State Enterprise has wrecked the people's self-reliance and initiative. As soon as a man gets out of work now his first aim is to demand that the State make him a billet. This, of course, the State cannot do, and the rejected job- seekers, who are growing in numbers daily, are like a lot of hornets round the ears of Ministers.

"There is one way out of the difficulty, and that is, the abandonment of the whole system of State Socialism and the re-establishment of private enterprise. If that policy were to be endorsed to-morrow, plenty of capital would be found for many schemes that are held up at present, and Ministers would be relieved of all worry and responsibilities. But they're not game, they're just hanging on—hanging on, and, I tell you, something is going to snap somewhere, sometime.

"From a military point of view there is no reason to worry. We have a big army in Egypt on the road to back you up, with more to follow. I must not say much on that matter. The censor will chop it out, but we're coming to the point that every man who doesn't go to the front must learn how to shoot straight. Let's hope he'll also learn that he can do a good deal to help fellows like yourself that are keeping the flag flying abroad, by keeping up confidence and the flag flying at home."

I read the letter to Nap.

"There are two points in that letter," he said. "The funk at home and the readiness to enlist. We've also got that funk-bee, sure. Why, when I left U.S.A. a ten million dollar war tax was launched, unemployed were swarming into the cities, factories were closing down because of the falling-off of exports, and the situation was getting so desperate that the Wilson-Bryan crowd were talking of forcing the British blockade of Germany with ships of contraband stuff. But there's no readiness to enlist, Jefson, not on your life. I'm sorry to say the physically worst are offering themselves for their country's service, and only ten per cent. of those offering are accepted; and though they advertise 'bowling alleys,' 'free trips round the world,' and other stunts as inducements, the response is so flat that when I passed through Chicago last August to come here, the recruiting stations had a notice up 'colored men wanted for infantry!' You know there's a sure prejudice against the nigger, we grudge giving him a vote, but when it comes to fighting for the country, well, he's as welcome as the 'flowers that bloom in the spring, tra-la.' I guess you Australians lick us right there."

"Information had been received of a new type of Zeppelin."—Chapter VIII.

CHAPTER VIII.

A Prisoner in Cologne.

A military operation order is crystallised commonsense. It is a wonderfully concise bunch of phraseology.

Our squadron commander read the latest by lamplight over a spread map of the theatre of war.

The general situation of the campaign explained that a Zeppelin raid on the east coast of England had been made on the 19th of January, thirteen days before.

Information had been received that a new type of Zeppelin had been constructed, a "mother" type, capable of carrying a number of aeroplanes.

The intention of the operation order was to destroy all known Zeppelin sheds; each air squadron supplying special officers for the purpose.

I well remember the particulars of that order. They printed their details upon my memory because I had been selected to destroy the sheds at Saarbruck. I was to leave three hours before the following dawn.

I remember Nap's disappointment that I was to go alone. He helped my machine out without a word. He may have had a premonition that I was not to return as I watched him silently fixing the compass and map-roller, testing the spring catch and guide of the bomb-dropper and packing into it its heavy load of "cough-drops." Then he stood like a dumb figure waiting for my starting signal.

"Buck up, Nap," I ventured, climbing into the seat. "One would think this was a funeral. I must get a hustle on as I've got to do 120 miles before I can get to business, so if everything's right, I'll swoop up."

Nap looked up.

"Fly high, and good luck," was all he said as he gripped my hand. Then I pressed the starter, the propeller hummed and pulled me into the star-specked sky.

I steered easterly, leaving on my left the red fire-glow of Rheims and passing over the sleepy lights of Valny. Within an hour I was over the great black stretch of the Argonne Forest, and crossing the Meuse, a long line of fog with Verdun 7000 feet below. The engine was working well, throwing back the miles at about 60 per hour. A glow of lights to the right showed Metz next to a streak of grey, the Moselle River; and as the dawn-light came into the sky, the Saar River came under me, covered by a fog with a fringe that flapped over its right bank and covered Saarbruck.

According to the sketch-map the Zeppelin sheds were near the railway station. So I flew low into the mist to get their correct position. The noise of my engine brought a shot from an aerial gun, but the fog saved me. A bunch of lights brought the station into view with the unmistakable long hangar of the Zeppelin adjacent to it.

I turned to get the sheds beneath me, and three foot-treads sent as many bombs chasing each other earthwards.

The first hit the ground near the shed, exploding without doing any damage. The second crashed through the roof of the hangar, its explosion being almost coincident with a fearful crash; the resulting air-rush almost overturning my 'plane. The third bomb fell into the back end of the shed, but I guessed it was not required.

My job was done, so I rose high above the fog line to get a straight run for home. Three Taubes were patrolling high, evidently on the look out.

I saw they would have the drop on me, so I sank back into the fog and under its cover swooped across the river for home. I was over the enemy's country where I guessed I was being searched for, so taking advantage of the fog I maintained a 1000 feet level and made a bee-line for Epernay.

THE ZEPPELIN SHED, AT SAARBRUCK.
Chapter VIII.

THE ZEPPELIN SHED, AT SAARBRUCK.
Chapter VIII.

My job was done, and I remember I was particularly elated.

I got a surprise near the Argonne Forest, striking a breeze that suddenly came up from the south, lifting the fog curtain and showing me dangerously close to the earth.

I swiftly jerked the elevator for a swoop up as a rifle cracked. I was spotted!

A volley of shots followed and—I was winged.

I remember, like a hideous dream, a long, evil-smelling shed in which I lay, a stiffly stretched and bandaged figure on a straw-strewn floor.

I was afterwards told it was Mezieres Railway Station, and that I was one of many hundred wounded being taken from the field hospitals to the base.

I need not detail my experiences for the next six months. I was taken from the hospital at Aix-la-Chapelle to Cologne to be attached to a gang of prisoners for street cleaning.

I remember our daily march across the Great Rhine Bridge with its wonderful arches at its entrance, and the great bronze horses on its flanks. I had occasion to remember that bridge, for there, some time later, the sunshine was to come into my life.

For six months I had not heard much of the war. My hospital friends had been wounded about the same time as I. My street-gang mates, a Belgian and a Frenchman, knew little except that up till June the Ostend-Nancy fighting line was still held by both armies. The lack of news did not worry me during my days of pain, but as the strength came back to me it brought a craving for news of the Great Game. Where were the Allies? What of the North Sea Fleet? How was Australia taking it? What was Nap doing? were questions that chased each other through my mind. Five Taubes had flown over us the day before, going south, but—what was doing?

It was on the Cologne Bridge a week later that a rather pretty girl, with an unmistakable English face, stopped to converse with one of my guard. At the same time she pointed to me: at which the guard looked round, frowned and spat with contempt.

"Are you English?" she queried.

"Yes," I replied, "I'm from Australia."

I had touched a sympathetic chord and she "sparked" up.

"Australia! Do you know Sydney?" she asked.

"I'm from Manly," was all I replied.

Then she did what I thought was a foolish thing—she came over and nearly shook my arm off!

The officer of the guard resented it, but she jabbered at him and explained to me that Australian prisoners were to have special treatment, then glancing at my number she stepped out across the bridge.

I found she was correct. When my gang returned to the barracks my number was called and I was questioned by the officer in charge. I was informed that Germany had no quarrel with Australia, hence I was only to be a prisoner on parole, to report myself twice a day and come and go as I pleased.

That is how I came to win great facts regarding Germany and her ideals. That is how I found out how it was that with Austria, Germany for nine months could hold at bay the mighty armies of the world's three greatest Empires, British, French and Russian, as well as the fighting cocks of Belgium; and at the same time endeavor to knock into some sort of fighting shape the crooked army of the Turks; how three nations of 109,000,000 people could defy for nine months the six greatest nations in the world with a joint population of 622,200,000!

The facts are of striking import to-day and should be understood by every man who is fighting for the Allies on and in the land, sea and air.

"On the bridge across the Rhine, at Cologne."—Chapter VIII.

CHAPTER IX.

Some Surprises in Cologne.

My unexpected freedom in Cologne was but one of many surprise.

There was the surprise of meeting an Australian friend in such unexpected quarters. I ascertained her name was Miss Goche. Her father was a well-known merchant of Melbourne, but was now living in Sydney. He had sent his daughter to the Leipsic Conservatorium to receive the technical polish every aspiring Australian musician seems to consider the "hall mark of excellence."

But the war closed the Conservatorium as it did most other concerns, by drawing out the younger professors to the firing line and the older men to the Landstrum, a body of spectacled elderly men in uniform, who felt the spirit wake in their feeble blood and prided themselves as "bloodthirsty dogs," as they watched railway lines, reservoirs, power stations, and did other unexciting small jobs.

Miss Goche was staying with her aunt and grandfather in Cologne. At their home I was made welcome.

Little restriction was placed on my movements, than the twice daily reporting at the Barracks.

I wondered at this freedom.

"It is easily explained," said old Goche, who could speak English. "The Fatherland knows no enmity with Australia. We have sympathy for the Indians, Canadians and other races of your Empire, who have been whipped into this war against their own free will."

"But," I interrupted, "there has been no whipping."

"Tut, tut," he continued. "We of the Fatherland know. Have we not proof? Our "Berliner Tageblatt" tells us so. We have no quarrel with the colonial people. Our hate is for England alone; and when this war is over and we have England at our feet, we shall be welcomed by Australia and the colonies, and we shall let them share with us the freedom and the light and the wisdom of our great Destiny."

There was no convincing the old man to the contrary, and his granddaughter informed me that the same opinion was universal in Germany.

"The best proof that it is so is the freedom you enjoy," she said.

"And yet there are times," she continued, "that I feel there is a subtle reason for this apparent kindliness for the colonies of the British Empire. You know Germany cannot successfully develop her own colonies. She has not that spirit of initiative that the Britisher has in attacking the various vicissitudes that every pioneer meets with in the development of a new land. That is why she let her colonies be snapped up by Australia without a pang; that is why as you say, she let her people hand over Rabaul and New Guinea to your Colonel Holmes without a battle. She fancies that when she wins this war as she has convinced herself she will, it will be a simple matter to step into the occupation of ready made colonies of such wonderful wealth and development."

The chief surprise of my freedom, however, was my changed opinion regarding the way Germany was taking the war.

I, like the average Britisher, had believed that in checking the German rush on Paris and driving it to the Aisne, we had whipped Germany to a standstill.

We had pictured her checked on the east with her Austrian ally on the verge of pleading for peace; her fleet cowering in the Kiel Canal like a frightened hen beneath a barn.

I, like every other Britisher, had fancied that Germany was undergoing an awful process of slow death; that she was faced with economic ruin; that her trade and manufacture had been smashed, causing untold ruination and forcing famine into every home; that the German populace were being crushed under the terrors of defeat, were cursing "the Kaiser and his tyrannical militarism," and waiting for the inevitable uprising with revolution and general social smash up.

And I knew such was the belief of the Allies and the world generally.

Never was a more mistaken notion spread!

Germany, notwithstanding what blunders and miscalculations she was accused of making, believed she would win.

This belief obsessed her.

Every movement, whether it achieves its direct object or not was made to nail that belief more secure.

A great philosopher wrote many years ago the following maxims:—

"To the persevering—everything is possible."

"They will conquer who believe they can."

Germany believed she would conquer, and for forty years she had been building up that belief.

"German aeroplanes were built from English types."
Chapter X.

CHAPTER X.

"Made in Germany."

Grandpa Goche told the story of Germany's development with mingled pride, yet with a tinge of regret.

We sat before his wide fireplace where a great fire crackled.

Puffing at his long pipe Grandpa Goche peered into the fire for a space before answering my query as to Germany's destiny.

"The destiny of the Deutschland?" he finally exclaimed. "Ah! It will be great and wonderful. But where it will end—who knows! Will it be like the Tower of Babel, great in conception, great in execution, but overreaching in its greatness? Will our destiny be like the snowball, accumulating as it rolls till it becomes immovable in its immensity? Then—stagnation! And yet the start of that snowball was but 50 years ago.

"I remember as a boy when Bismarck was Prime Minister of Prussia, and he forced through the Reichstag his great army re-organisation scheme. In '64 he attacked Denmark and took Schleswig-Holstein. That is how we got Kiel. Two years after he crushed the Austrians in six weeks, and took Hanover, Hesse, and Nassau; and four years after that he smashed the French and took Alsace-Lorraine.

"Flushed with victory, proud Deutschland, with Denmark, Austria and France humbled in the dust, wiped her sword and peered at the Dawn. But she did not sheath that sword. No! In the ecstasy of triumph she was trying to formulate a policy of carving a destiny great and glorious. She looked first to peaceful development by legislation; and then, in that passing period of uncertainty, Bismarck threw out his famous declaration that the destiny of Deutschland was to be won, not by votes and speeches, but by Blood and Iron.

"It was what you call a 'happy hit.'

"It appealed to the animal strength of the German race. Bismarck knew that beneath the surface most of the men of Germany were of a wild nature; he knew that in less than a century they rose from the degradation of conquered barbarians to the heights of victors of three nations, and the 'blood and iron' policy ran through Germany as a new inspiration.

"Bismarck floated the great new Ship of State, and stood at the wheel peering keenly into the troublous waters of the future. There was one great rock of which he wished to steer clear, so on the Ship of Destiny he placed a maxim.

It was: 'War not with England.'

"There were other simple rules of navigation that irritated a new young officer on the bridge, who felt that the Bismarckian policy, though perhaps sure, was not speedy enough for his vaulting ambition.

"I remember well this young Kaiser, a man of wonderful vitality, who revelled in the strength of developing manhood, and who early began to assert himself. Those who tried to curb his youthful impetuosity went down before him till there was but one great personality left who could talk to him as a father would to his wayward son. It was Bismarck, he who dragged Prussia from the depths and gave her the ideal for a world power. The cool calculating wiseacre said, 'Steady, lad,' so—he had to go.

"Then the Kaiser took the wheel.

"He found Germany a comparatively small country, with a great and prolific population of sixty-six millions. He found the German woman not the mild and simple 'hausfrau' of folk lore, but a virile woman with a creed that the production of children was her first duty, not only to her husband and herself, but to her country. He knew that in Germany illegitimacy was no disgrace, and he saw Germany's population increase ten millions in the course of ten years.

"He looked at his restricted boundaries and saw his people being bottled up. That's why he gave the declaration that 'Germany's destiny is upon the water'.

"We needed colonies, but all the colonies worth having were taken by— whom? Your England!

"We were hungry for trade and influence in distant waters, but your England held the gateways to the world's trade channels.

"The road to Asia and Australia was lined with England's forts, and Gibraltar, Malta, Port Said and Aden watched the way like frowning sentinels.

"It was then that we prepared for 'The Day.'

"Our Kaiser gave the call 'Deutschland Uber Alles' (Germany over all). It was a new creed, and it soon gained the strength of a religion.

"I know you English ridicule the idea of the Kaiser and his Divine Right—but do not forget an English King claimed the same thing."

"DROPPING THE PILOT."
Tenniel's Cartoon in "Punch," showing the reckless irresponsibility of the
Kaiser began early.

"Yes," I interrupted, "and we chopped off his head."

He went on, ignoring my interruption—

"You English speak of God as the God of Hosts and the God of Battles, but you only mouth it. We Germans believe in it, and we work for it. It permeates our life like a divine call. It makes every man feel he is a part of a great whole, a working unit in an immense machine, whether it be in the field of battle or in the field of industry. We feel we are doing a divine duty.

"And this divine spirit is in our work.

"We associate all our tasks with a sense of service to our fellow citizens. We make trade and civic education compulsory to all boys from 14 to 18 years of age and to all girls from 11 to 16 years of age. Your England has only 26 per cent. of children at school between those ages.

"We train our children and people to discharge specialised functions. We associate practice with theory. We amalgamate science with manufacture.

"Your England at one time was the chief glass manufacturing country, but thirty years ago a professor of mathematics at Jena joined a glass maker, and to-day we lead in the world's glass manufacture.

"In 1910, your England exported one and a half million pounds worth of glass, and Germany exported five million pounds worth.

"In 1880, your England led the world in the output of pig iron, producing nearly eight million tons to four million tons produced by the United States.

"In 1910, the United States produced twenty-seven million tons, Germany fifteen million tons, and Great Britain ten million tons.

"In 1856 an Englishman named Perkins first produced a coal tar dye.

"In 1910, Germany exported nine and a half million pounds worth, while Great Britain exported only £336,000 worth.

"So you see Germany has beaten England in peace as you will see we shall beat her in war."

Then he spat into the fire, put his pipe away, and as he was going out to bed flung this final shot:

"And there again we differ from you English. That is why we go into this divine struggle as a grim and serious business. One great united army with a hymn to God, and one great battle cry, 'Deutschland Uber Alles.' You English take it as what you call 'a jolly sport,' with your battle cry, 'Are we down-hearted?' and your battle hymn, 'It's a long long way to Tipperary,' ah-ha-ho"—and he laughed his way up to his bedroom.

I sat looking into the dying flames, dwelling upon all his jibes.

I thought how each German felt he was a cog in the immense national machine, and had his work systematised. I could then understand how that killed initiative in the individual, and why Germany had not made any great discoveries in science or manufacture, but had simply stolen ideas of other countries and adapted them to her own ends.

Grandpa Goche had spoken of coal tar dye, then I recalled how Germany had also taken Marconi's wireless invention and Germanised it; how it had taken the French and the English ideas in airship and aeroplane construction and worked upon them; how even the English town planning movement was imitated. In the latter case I remembered reading that the "Unter den linden" had been widened by the process of pushing the dwellings back until they each housed 60 families. Germany, on this occasion, had grabbed the idea but missed the spirit, in the absence of which town planning is merely a name.

Even the manufactures of Germany had been built upon those of other countries. There was a case I recalled, that of the Australian cordial manufacturer, who desired to introduce his stuff into Germany. He was met with a stiff tariff, but informed that if he established a factory there there would be no need to import it. Why, now I came to remember it, even the original "Rush-on-Paris" plan was stolen. Hilaire Belloc, the Anglicised Frenchman, had written of it in the "London" Magazine, of May, 1912. When that plan failed what had Germany done? Why, dug itself in on the Aisne!

The idea of the German submarine raids was not original, as it formed the base of a story by Sir Conan Doyle that appeared in the English "Strand Magazine" and in the American "Colliers' Weekly" many months before!

Germany, in fact, built its fame on assiduous imitation rather than originality. But at what cost? Its people had degenerated in the process from thinking humans to dumb, driven cattle, going, going, for ever going, but non-comprehending the why or the wherefore of it all, beyond the arrogant assumption of "welt-politik." Every refining trait was subordinated to the exigencies of the gospel of force. Not only the plebeian mass, but the exclusive aristocracy, revelled in the brutish impulse that associated all appeals to reason with effeminacy and invested the sword-slash on the student's cheek with the honor ordinarily claimed by the diploma.

This gospel of exalting animal strength developed a living passion for tyranny and grossness. We have seen it evidenced in the orgies that have reddened Belgium and France.

And I had given my parole to a nation without a soul—a nation that expected honor but knew not what it meant.

I crept to bed disturbed in mind, but resolved next day to take certain action.

“I remembered our march across the great Rhine Bridge, with its wonderful arches and great bronze horses.”—Chapter VIII.

CHAPTER XI.

The Escape from Cologne.

Next morn I rose from a sleepless couch.

Thoughts grim and gaunt had purged my brain the whole night long. There was a flood of reasons why I should leave that German home. I chafed at being a guest in the house of old Goche, whose animosity to the Cause was undying. I could see that our discussions on the war were increasing in bitterness and would, ere long, terminate in a storm. I desired to avoid this for the sake of Miss Goche, whose friendship was the only balm in that period of stress. I had little further desire to accept hospitality from a stranger simply because I happened to be from the same country as his granddaughter.

But greatest of all reasons why I should leave was because I had now completely recovered from my wound, and the War of the World was waging within 100 miles of me.

My job was "action on the firing line" and not lolling in security as a guest of an enemy! Now that my wound had healed and my strength had knitted firmly again, I felt I was a traitor in giving my parole not to escape.

That August morning, when I made my first daily call at the barracks, I stated to the officer to whom I generally reported, that I was going to try and escape. He first seemed somewhat surprised, but soon broke into a laugh. Turning, he spoke laughingly to another officer, who joined in the hilarity.

"So you're going to escape, eh?" he said. "Well, we don't think you will. If you intended to escape you would not be so foolish as to tell us about it; and then, if you did attempt it, you could not get out of Cologne with an English face like yours. That's alright," he repeated, "you will report this afternoon as usual."

I stood awhile.

"There is the door," he said. "Good morning, we are busy."

I returned and acquainted Miss Goche of my action.

I explained there were two reasons for my giving notice. I could now attempt to get away without breaking my parole; and now no blame could be placed on the Goche household for my escape.

I need not here mention the scene that followed, but I may state I was aware that my departure had taken on a new aspect. I knew I was leaving one for whom I had now more than friendship, one whom I found had risked much to make me secure. She admitted that, without doubt, my duty lay beyond the Rhine.

"But you will please me greatly if you will report at the barracks this afternoon, as usual," she said.

I did so, and was met by an officer with an "I told you so" smile.

I left the Goche home that afternoon at dusk. I did not intend to cross the river at Cologne. The way west would be too black with grim forebodings. The best opportunity of escaping seemed to be south, down the right bank of the Rhine to Coblenz, then crossing to the Rhine mountains, going south into Luxembourg, and then keeping east, trusting to good fortune to get through the German lines into the Vosges.

Miss Goche accompanied me as far as the park on the river bank, where in a quiet alcove I somewhat Germanised my appearance. I shaved my short beard and trimmed my moustache with the ends erect, the now universal fashion of the German menfolk; and with an old felt cap and unmistakable German clothes, I felt I could probably pass muster until I opened my mouth.

I had, thanks to my good friend, learned off a few German phrases for use at odd times, so, as night fell we parted.

Down the pathway I stepped with a world of mystery ahead of me. I remember now it took no slight effort to leave, but though the call away was unmistakable, I knew the reply was the hardest task in my experience. But I set my teeth and trudged down the track till I reached the bend, then I looked back. At the top of the road a figure stood, a hand waved and—yes—a kiss was thrown, then she turned away.

I felt alone in a new world, so marked my way and went into the night.

During the first hours I stepped along in fear and trembling. I peopled every dark corner with a sentry; I pictured every distant tree as covering watching soldiers. I wondered at the lack of challenge, till it dawned upon me that I was not in the fighting country. There was no war in these parts, so I tramped along at the side of the road till early morning, the only incident being a hail from a man on a bridge which I had passed but did not have to cross. The bridges were evidently guarded. As dawn light came into the sky I saw an aeroplane pass flying low and stared at by an early morning ploughman, then I crept behind a hedge and stole a sleep.

CHAPTER XII.

The Waste of War.

I could not have been long in slumber, when a slight noise, perhaps the cracking of a stick, drove sleep from my anxious brain, and I sat up with surprise, staring at a long figure in black that stood peering at me. The black gown, the beads and the broad-brimmed hat told me it was a priest.

He spoke to me in German. It was one of the sentences Miss Goche told me I would be asked—he wished to know where I was going. So I fired at him a second of my readied German phrases: "I'm going south to fight," I said, which was true.

Then he let free a flood of German that floored me. He waited for a reply that hesitated; then with a queried look into my face, he said: "English! you're no German," and his eyes began to twinkle.

"You can confess," he said, "remember there is no war with men of God. I, too, am going south, I am going to France, our journey will seem quicker in company, let us step forth."

He was a Christian Brother. He had been to Australia, where many of his Order were established. I explained I knew of their work in education; in fact, I happened to know many of the fraternity by name. I ran over a gamut of names of those I knew in past years. There were Brothers Paul, Wilbrid, Aloysius and Mark.

"I may know some of those you mention," he said, "but I do not think it possible. We seldom know each other by name unless we are beneath the same roof. There are hundreds called by the names you mentioned, I myself am a 'Brother Wilbrid.'"

It is a wonderful fact that there is nothing that knits strangers together, as the hitting on the name of a mutual friend, so we became close companions.

He had been born in Lorraine, but had lived most of his time in Berlin. His close-cropped grey hair showed he was well on in years. He had been an artisan before he joined his Order, and he lightened our long tramp to Coblenz with his idea of the trend of things.

The road was good and the air was clean and sweet. We passed by some farms where women were behind the plough.

Summer was breaking, and the Autumn sunshine was drying the last dewdrops from the grass.

"Note," Brother Wilbrid said, "how all Nature welcomes the sunshine, hear the birds twitter, see the cattle slowly moving on that rise. All Nature here joins in a hymn of peace, yet far beyond those western ridges three million men lay trenched through the winter and stared in hellish hate at each other across a narrow strip.

"All Nature welcomed the Spring with a pæan of praise, but by fighting men it was welcomed as the opportunity to rise from winter holes and rush across the Spring sun-warmed earth to warm it anew with flowing blood. But it is not the waste of blood that so appals, it's the waste of effort and the waste of heroism. The labor of three million men could, in the wasted months of war build much to ensure unending human happiness. Thirty-two thousand men cut a channel through Panama and shortened the world's journey to your home by a third! Think what the labor of three million men could do!

"And then there is the waste of heroism.

"Men with large hearts will risk their lives to drag a comrade out of danger. It is heroism—yes—but it is wasted on a cause of foolishness——"

"But," I interrupted, "there is other heroism than that on the fighting line," and I told him the story of Abbe Chinot, of Rheims, the young priest in charge of the cathedral; how, when German shells were crashing into the grand old pile which was being used as a hospital for German soldiers, Chinot, aided by Red Cross nurses, dragged the wounded into the street, where surged a mob, maddened that their beloved church was in flames, and that their homes and five hundred of their folks had been smashed with German shells. The sight of the grey uniforms on the German wounded drove the mob into frenzied screams of revenge, but the fearless Abbe placed himself between the uplifted rifles of the crowd and the German wounded. "If you kill them," he said, "you must first kill us"; and how the mob, struck with his perfect courage, moved away in silence.

THE CATHEDRAL OF RHEIMS.

"Smashed with German Shells."
(The Rheims Cathedral Front.)]

"Yes, that is fine, very fine," he said—"yet it does not prove that the war made the brave Abbe heroic.

"This war is unnecessary. It is the most unnecessary of all wars. It is not a war of the people. It is a merchants' war. It is not a war of the workers. It is a war for commerce—and four million or more lives will go up to God in the interests of Trade.

"I fear the consequences of this war. I feel this war spirit will bring on a sequel that will surprise humanity.

"A great writer[1] likened the war spirit to a carbuncle on the body. The poison flowing through the blood localises itself, and a painful lump forms in the flesh. Relief is sought in salves, ointments, and poultices. But the lump continues to swell, and the pain to increase, until at the very time when the soul is in mortal agony the carbuncle bursts and spews out the poison. The pain ceases, the swelling subsides, and the flesh regains its normal color.

"The poison of injustice flows through the veins of society. Men are denied their natural rights; and when the oppression becomes unendurable, their oppressors make all manner of excuses. The affliction is due, they say, to the wrath of God, to the niggardliness of nature, or to the encroachments of foreign nations. Ah, the encroachments of foreign nations! When all other excuses fail, there is this to fall back upon; and each ruling class of oppressors holds its victims in subjection by charging the trouble to the others.

"But the people are awakening. A few already see their real oppressors. It is for each who sees the truth to tell his fellow, and that fellow his fellow, until presently all will know the truth, and the truth shall make them free; free from industrial tyranny at home, and free from military tyranny from abroad. The work of the peace advocate is not negative. It is not enough for him to cry peace, peace! He must first lay the foundation for peace. To cry peace while the people writhe under injustice is like trying to heal the carbuncle without cleansing the blood."

[1] Stoughton Cooley.

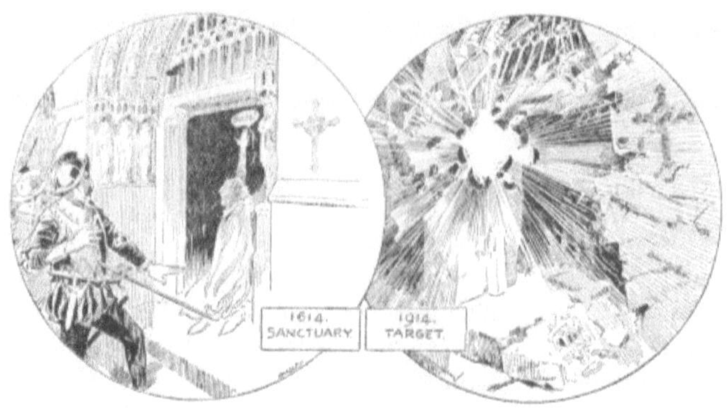

"The Waste of War."—Chapter XII.
(The Cartoon, "Advance of Civilisation," by Bradley, in the "Chicago Daily Mail.")

"The Waste of War."—Chapter XII.
(The Cartoon, "Advance of Civilisation," by Bradley, in the "Chicago Daily Mail.")

"It is not the people's fight."—Chapter XIII.
(The Cartoon, "Must Peace Wait for This," by Bradley, in the "Chicago Daily Mail.")

"It is not the people's fight."—Chapter XIII.
(The Cartoon, "Must Peace Wait for This," by Bradley, in the "Chicago Daily Mail.")

CHAPTER XIII.

How the War Wrecked Theories.

I shall never forget that wonderful walk on the Coblenz road: the grave, hard-cut featured face of the man of religion, pouring out his socialistic theories, like a long pent-up torrent bursting through years of accumulated debris. At one moment he would be calm and clear, but at times, in his excitement, he would lash at wayside flowers with his stick like a soldier with a sabre.

"The people are not sincere at heart in this Great War," he said, "it is not the people's fight. If soldiers only had their own way this war would be short lasting—in fact the war nearly ended on Christmas Day. You have heard how the Germans and the English ceased firing at the dawn of that holy morn. How a bayonet from a German trench held up a placard with those magic words of good cheer that ever move the world—"A Merry Christmas." How each side sang hymns at the other's invitation, crossed the zone of fire, and exchanged cigarettes. Surely the spirits of Jesus and Jaures moved along that line that wonderful morn."

"And yet," I said, "when time was up, back to their trenches the soldiers crept and fought again like devils."

He went on, ignoring my interruption.

"And German officers, high in rank, held up their hands in horror at the idea of an armistice being arranged without their consent. That is the spirit that is going to end war—that human spirit that came to the surface on Christmas morn and that proved that this awful war is but a thing of Business."

Our road passed along the cliff tops of the Rhine. There was little traffic on the river and no sign of war. Everything seemed peaceful. The war, in draining the men and youths from the countryside, had placed a mantle of calm upon life in the villages of the Rhine Valley. Even across the river a long length of railway line lay as a long road of emptiness. Not a train, not a truck, not any sign of life was upon the long stretch of metal.

"And yet," said Brother Wilbrid, "that is the main line from Bonn to Coblenz. All railwaymen, stock, and traffic are confined to the Theatres of War."

We had walked in silence for quite a while. My companion was lost in thought. I ventured an interruption.

"You are a Socialist," I said.

He looked at me a while before replying.

"A Socialist? Well, no, I'm not—that is so far as Socialists have gone. I describe myself as a 'Humanist.' Socialism as we had it before the war was synonymous with revolution. Its creed, 'Revolution before evolution,' spelt destruction and anarchy. It aimed to get what it wanted by force instead of striving to get it by constitutional means. I broke with them just there—and yet—and yet," he mused, as if to himself, "they were hounded down as outlaws of society for promising force—for threatening to do what the armies are to-day doing in the 'interests of civilisation.'

"What a shuffle of theories this mighty conflict has brought about! Strange that your Allies claim they are fighting to save civilisation from being destroyed by the 'German barbarians,' whilst the German convinces himself that he is fighting to impress his 'higher culture' upon an unenlightened world!

"Listen! I was once an engineer in the Krupp Works, at Essen; that nest of the German War Eagle. I was but a unit in a mighty mass. We were all well treated. Our health was well served. Our masters had learned that, just as they watched the health of horses, it was just as necessary to study the well-being of their human workers; so model homes and villages were built for us, our masters realising that if we were healthy they would get more work from us. They were philanthropists with an eye on the output. And the average German worker was getting contented—getting into a groove."

"That Nest of the German War Eagle."-Chapter XIII.
(The Krupp Works, at Essen.)

"Then," I ventured, "if a man's contented and has nothing to growl about—why worry?"

"Ah," he replied, "that's just the trouble, the German worker, as a worker, has little to complain of, but he is becoming systematised. He cannot rise, he is forced to be content and do his job. His health is insured by groups of employers sharing the responsibility. If workers get hurt too much or sick too much, the insurance syndicate begins to lose money; hence safety devices are considered and sanitoria built to prevent illness; and this German social insurance speeds individual initiative to top speed. It makes the German worker a splendid animal—and there is the danger.

"You know it's human nature to complain—progress is built upon discomfort, contentment means stagnation. I could see the workers fixed in their contented groove under the studied philanthropy of his employers and ending as in the dumb-driven-cattle age of the Feudal Barons."

"It strikes me," I said, "that the Socialist is of that type of Irishman that's never happy unless there's a chance of a fight. You might at least admit that many employers have hearts like other human beings. There are many that recognise that profits are not everything."

"No doubt," he said, "but they're not in Germany. Prior to the war the workers were moving close to a war with employers—the rise of Labor has been steady and sure the world over. Why in your own country, Australia, Labor already controls the Governments. It was coming to that in Europe. The worker was climbing, climbing, all the time—organising, organising—but against the increasing demand for labor the employers had a powerful weapon in the invention of labor-saving machinery.

"Every day saw more and more of the work of the world taken up by machinery. Did a labor union demand increased wages, then a machine was devised to do the work with less assistance. In a return issued by the U.S. Government, it was estimated that 4,500,000 factory machine workers of that country were turning out products in quantities equal to the hand labor of 45,000,000 men. That meant that 90 per cent. of the work in factories was being done by machinery; that one man, with the help of machines could produce ten times more than he needs. It was more acute in Germany. In other words, to satisfy the wants of one man for one day, a factory worker with a machine requires only one hour instead of the ten he formerly worked. For whom was he doing the work of the remaining nine hours? Why, for rulers, soldiers, and other parasites, who do not work but have to live.

"When I was a worker in Essen I saw the set lives of the workers—noted how a new labor-saving device threw out so many men at a time. I looked back at the development of machinery and saw that a very large part of machinery is driven by steam-power, which meant largely coal-power, and I knew with the getting and burning of the coal there was not only a terrible waste of human labor, but 90 per cent. of the heat generated escaped unused, and not more than 5 per cent. of the stored energy in the coal became available for human needs. Even the finest quadruple expansion engines, with all the modern devices for super-heated steam to augment their capacity, did not utilise more than 15 per cent. We engineer workers knew that if an engine were invented to economise this waste there would be a further reduction of labor—and this device came. It came in the Diesel motor."

"This wonderful engine meant the production of power from crude oil at a cost of one-eighth of a penny to a farthing per horse-power, far beyond the economy of any other form of engine and five times cheaper than the ordinary steam engine. Its only rival was water-power—and water-power is not everywhere.

"We could see, at no distant day, nine-tenths of the workers of the world supplanted by the machine! We could see that new labor-saving machinery would mean a fearful catastrophe in the labor markets of the world. Think of it. We could see wonderful engines, put together by the hands of the workers in the factories, pushing out the useless laborer, pushing him out into the crowded avenues of unemployed. We could see this awful Frankenstein of machinery—a huge soulless metal monster, stalking through the world, bringing starvation, anarchy and destruction in its wake. 'It should not be—it must not be,' we said, and lots were drawn."

Then he stopped short and sat upon a bank at the roadside.

I watched him stare in thought at an ant creeping over a twig at his feet.

"Well?" I said.

He started and looked at me with lowered head. He peered at me beneath his long grey eyebrows and quietly whispered—"Diesel had to die."

"Then he was killed!" I said, starting up. I remembered he had mysteriously disappeared in October, 1913.

"Yes," he replied, "and it was my task."

He turned from me and looked across the peaceful Rhine. In the silence faint booms seemed to come from the western battlefield, but it may have been the throbbing of my brain. I looked at the man with his hard-set jaw and quivering lips.

I sat down again at his side, and for many minutes silently scratched lines upon the road.

Fully ten minutes passed, and he turned his face to me.

"Listen!" he said. "Can you hear those distant guns? They tell me there's no Socialism in the world to-day. That war came in and smashed the barriers. At Ghent, not long before the war, an International Congress met and formed an

Association for the best development of the world's cities; at Paris, one month before the strife broke out, 2000 delegates from Chambers of Commerce, representing 31 nations, met to ensure the world's commercial peace and commercial prosperity; and just before the war a World's Congress of Socialists met in Berlin, and Jaures won every heart with his denunciation of human strife.

"Within a month a city-destroying army passed through Ghent and wrecked the greatest constructional glories of the world. Within a month the world's commerce was paralysed. Within a month Jaures was shot and Socialists the world over became blood-blinded. To-day they 'see red.' They know not what they are fighting for, but there they fight like bloodthirsty fiends because they're told to. What are they fighting for? Will life be any harder for them what flag flies above their city? The people fight and the people suffer, and when their job is done those left are given scraps of metal to wear and are sent back to clear up the mess."

"Stop!" I said. "Don't forget there is such a thing as Patriotism. Listen!

> "'Breathes there the man with soul so dead
> Who never to himself hath said,
> This is my own, my native land.'"

Then he looked at me for a moment with his grave grey face—and smiled.

"Listen, my boy, I am not a Frenchman, though born in Lorraine—I am not a German, though living most of my life in Germany—I am a Worldsman. I am a Christian. To me all men are as brothers. I do not love any country more than any other. I prove that by making a friend of you. I should, in the casual order of things just now, hate you with the awful German hate of England. Patriotism is the love of the land in which you accidentally happened to be born. Why should any one love a particular geographical district upon the face of the earth because there he happened to first see the light?

"Let me tell you," he continued, with a strange fire in his eyes and slashing at a flower by the way, "God, or Nature if you like, will enact a punishment to fit this awful crime of the murder of five million men, and the heartbreaks of mothers, wives and children. This, the greatest tragedy the world has ever seen, will call for a fearful atonement. I foresee, in this war, with its daily expense of three million pounds, and the additional waste, a general bankruptcy of the world, the downfall of classes, of wealth, the wrecking of privilege. I foresee, when peace is declared, the fruitless return of millions of men to jobs that have vanished, and to employers shorn of all power to employ them. Mark me! The world to-day is on the verge of a mighty cataclysm far greater than the present awful clash of armies. Wise are the man and country that are preparing."

He paused awhile as if in deep thought.

"Listen, my boy, you quoted me some verse just now, let me quote you lines from the new version of the 'Watch on the Rhine':

> "Dear Fatherland, we'll soon be free,
> From Prussian Kings' autocracy:
> The world shall see all the battles cease,
> With dawn of universal peace.
> Each German worker has to pay
> One-fourth of what he earns per day
> To keep two million marching feet
> And please a Kaiser's mad conceit.
> Oh God! we're punished bitterly
> For Kaiser Wilhelm's blasphemy;
> Three million of our sons are slain,
> Let sacrifice be not in vain!"

He rose abruptly, grasped his stick, and set off down the road.

I stood for a moment half-dazed; then I followed him.

"If soldiers only had their own way, this war would be short lasting."—
Chapter XIII.
(The Cartoon, "An International Conference that would bring about Peace,"
by Bradley, in the "Chicago Daily News.")

CHAPTER XIV.

The Restless Masses.

What sort of man was this? "A man of God" and yet a murderer! A man without a spark of patriotism. A man without a country. What a curiosity in these days, when at the first blast of war almost every man on earth ranged himself beneath a nation's flag be it for strife or neutral!

Here was a man:—

> Whose heart had ne'er within him burned,
> As home his footsteps he had turned,
> From wandering on a foreign strand—

And the rhyming lines kept jogging through my brain as I trudged behind that long straight figure in black.

A turn of the road brought a house in sight and my companion quickened his steps. I hung back as he went up to the house. He turned, looked around, and waved me on. I passed by and waited some distance along the road.

An hour later he came up. He brought some brown bread and salt meat to me, and even better, some news of what was doing; and he told it to me as I sat and ate upon the bank. I remember, as he talked, and I kept watching far to the west where some aeroplanes hovered above the now greening tops of the forest hills.

"You get the truth from country folk," he said. "They win their news first hand from wounded fathers and sons. In the city the war news is ground, sifted, and only what is of little interest is dispersed. There have been great deeds. The German armies hold the line between Ghent and Mulhausen and are wearing out the Allies by exhaustion. Many armies have reinforced the British and the French, but the German lines hold fast and wear out the Allies. The Russians are still upon the defensive in Poland. London is in a panic as it has been attacked by Zeppelins, and the German Fleet has come out from Kiel and claims a victory. That news, of course, you can doubt, as it does not come first hand. The Allies, however, threaten Constantinople and the Turkish armies are demoralised. But the greatest of the news," and here the fire came into his face again, "is that the workers of the world are uneasy. Strikes rage in England, in Australia, in Canada, in the United States, and—yes in Germany. The English shipyard workers on the Clyde and at Southampton have at various times since March held up British naval construction; and it is now August. There is a universal demand for shorter hours with increased wages, and food prices are high. The Australian workers are striking against their own Labor Governments, and refusing to fit out troopships unless they get treble pay for night work, and in Germany the workers are rising because they are tiring of forced employment. All the civil, as well as military factories, have been working treble shifts; and huge stocks of all kinds of manufactures have accumulated everywhere and cannot be distributed. Workers are losing heart. This war is stretching out too long for them. It was to be a short, sharp war, and they now fear time is on the side of the Allies, so a general uprising is threatened. But alas—alas!" he continued as if to himself, "this news is a fortnight old."

Then he turned to me with anxious face.

"I knew not of these things when I went on this road to Coblenz," he said. "For fourteen days I had been in silent seclusion in a monastery at Deutz, as each of our brotherhood must do once a year; and now I must retrace my steps. I feel this new rebellion is a call to me. Listen, my new found friend," and he peered into my face. "I left the world two years ago. I could see that a change in great human conditions was inevitable. I was what you call a labor leader. I went into a monastery for two purposes. I can confess to you. It is safe, as we will never meet again, and all ideas of justice will upend in the coming cataclysm. Listen I say," and he gripped my wrist with a vice-like clutch of his bony fingers. "I went into a monastery to escape the suspicion that I had removed one whom we felt would bring much unhappiness upon the earth. I went into a monastery to think. The turmoil of a busy worker's life gave little opportunity for serious thought. I felt the day was coming when the workers of the world would rise. I wanted to study the proposition and its possibilities with all the clearness of vision that the calmness of a monastery could give. I feel now that the day is coming fast. It is near. All the signs of the approaching storm are being manifested. I am ready.

"Some clear-visioned people in high office saw the portents in the sky and feared the toppling of the thrones, so threw this war into the ring to give the toilers opportunity for their heated passions, but this war will be like blood to a tiger, it will quicken up the fighting spirit of the animal, and on those who forced this war it will recoil with awful effect. They saw the labor storm approach and put off the evil day. It was like neglecting to physic the human body—the longer deferred, the worse the disease.

"I am going back again," he continued. "You had better go on into France. Your trouble will be to cross the Rhine."

He paused awhile and looked pityingly at me.

"Alas!" he continued. "You're a poor fool in these wild parts with only your English and your bad French."

He took a sheet of paper from his pocket and sketched a rough map upon it.

"You can cross the Rhine," he went on, "just here at Neuwied, it is but a mile along this road, then you go directly west to the Coblenz-Treves Road, which follows the Mozelle. That road will take you to Luxembourg; but keep away from Coblenz. They tell me at the farmhouse that it is full of wounded soldiers and others are coming in by the Treves railway that skirts the road you will take. Beyond the Rhine there is much danger to you, but take this," and he wrote some words on the back of the map. "God pardon me, for I know it is not all truth. Those words are German—they say you are 'deaf and dumb' and that 'you are going to the front.'"

"Then you are going back to Cologne?" I asked.

"Yes," he said, "and beyond. I know not yet—perhaps to Berlin."

A distant bell chimed.

"The Angelus," he said, standing and bowing his head in prayer. Though not of his religion I also removed my hat and stood beside that man of deep mystery. His steel grey hair and care-lined face seemed foreign to his strong built frame and iron hand grip, and as he prayed upon the road, my thoughts rolled back to Cologne and dwelt upon that brave girl whose friendship had made so sweet my prison days in that City of the Bridges. I pictured my last vision of her upon the hill, wafting me a farewell.

The man of prayer interrupted my reverie.

"It is now good-bye, Australian," he said. "Though all countries are alike to me, your nation seems to promise much. It leads the world in justice for the men who toil, and perhaps that is why I would like to see you safely out of this maelstrom of human passions; but our ways must part just here—good- bye!"

He left me as the evening shadows began to encircle the hills, and though I felt a strange feeling of loneliness as he passed up the road and out of sight, I felt brave and cheerful—for my friend had taken a love-letter to Cologne for me.

CHAPTER XV.

Figures on the Road.

I reached the Rhine at dusk. The ferry barge, a small rope affair with a hand wheel, was at the water's edge. All was quiet this side of the river, but across the water anxious voices called. Close to me a door opened and a shaft of light split the darkness as the little old and white-haired ferry keeper came clattering out, wiping his mouth and muttering savagely. He stepped upon the barge. I followed and took the wheel from him. He smiled and spoke, but as I pointed to my ears and tongue and shook my head, he nodded. Between us we worked the barge across the river.

As the ferry neared the bank my heart beat fast, for I saw the waiting figures were soldiers! There were five of them and they seemed impatient. Before the barge had touched the shore they had jumped aboard, not noticing me walk off. They were without rifles, this struck me at the time as very significant, and the soldiers began to hurriedly work the ferry back again. I turned and watched the barge fade into the darkness, but hearing footsteps, looked up and saw more soldiers outlined on the skyline of the high bank. The road zig- zagged up the hill, and by keeping in the shadow of the cliff I passed along without trouble. From the hilltop I discovered to the left the light-dotted city of Coblenz. I took the road to the west and walked through the night. At times many people passed along that road to the river, including scattered bands of soldiers. I knew them by their spiked helmets silhouetted against the sky.

It must have been midnight when I struck the main Coblenz Road. A string of waggons and carts rumbled along towards Coblenz with many soldiers walking between. Close by a railway line ran parallel with the road and continuous trains slowly crawled, hissing and shrieking like wounded things. I plodded along the tree-screened roadside, the cloudy darkness of the night helping my security. And all through that night and early morning silent tramping figures passed along—all going in the one direction!

As dawn began to break I left the high road, tired and foot weary and struck into the bush to snatch some sleep.

I woke with the sun well up in the sky. I still could hear the squealing of the railway trains, and when I climbed to a distant ridge and looked around me I saw the Coblenz-Treves road stretching far to the south-west and dotted with figures—grey soldiers and others, hospital waggons and farm carts, all moving along like a great procession.

I felt that road was not safe for me.

Beyond the belt of timber between myself and the road were fenced paddocks with scattered farm houses. To the west the forest stretched where far ahead a speck of white caught my eye. I made it a guide mark and worked towards it.

Beyond the ridge I stumbled on to a small farm, and as I came in sight a barking dog brought a woman to the door. I felt hungry and took a chance. She watched me approach, then closed the door, and as I came up she opened it again, but held a gun in her hand and talked fiercely at me.

I pointed to my ear and tongue and shook my head; at the same time held out the sheet of paper. I remember the simple old lady put down her gun and pulled the spectacles from her forehead to her nose, read my note that I was 'going to the front' and—kissed me! Possibly this was because of the suggestion of a retreat, whilst I, a mute, was going to the fighting line. Then she pointed towards the road and went off into a temper, rattling off a torrent of excited German, and again looking towards the road, spat vigorously.

As she handed me bread and cheese there were tears in her eyes. I remember as I left I kissed her and as I made for the strip of white I had seen earlier in the day, I carried the vision of those tear-dimmed eyes. "Somebody's mother," I mused. "Somebody's mother."

CHAPTER XVI.

From February to August.

It has been said that, if coincidences did not happen, stories would not be written, and what I am about to write seemed at first strange, and yet, as events proved, was only natural.

Before I reached the white mark upon the tree I heard the noise of the breaking of bushes, so I carefully reconnoitred, and before long a swishing near by caused me to drop beneath a shrub, as there passed me within one hundred yards a figure dragging two saplings. I clapped my hand over my mouth to prevent shouting. It looked like Nap!

In my excitement I had moved. A sun-ray struck my white jacket. The figure stood, dropped the bushes, drew his revolver and turned his face toward me. It was Nap!

I rushed out.

"Nap," I shouted—but the revolver was still pointed.

"Hands up," he called, nonplussed at the German-looking figure rushing towards him. I threw his old phrase at him: "Fly high and good luck, old man." Then his arm dropped.

"The voice is Jefson's, sure enough," he said, "but the darned mug licks me."

"Wait till I cover up the mo'," I said, putting my hand over my mouth.

"Well, old chap, shall we drop a 'cough drop'?" I asked; and he nearly wrung my arm off.

"I fell near here three nights ago," he explained, "engine trouble—and, although it's enemy's country I don't like to burn the old 'bus, so I've backed its tail as far as I could into the bush and am screening the exposed part with bushes so that it won't be spotted from aloft. There's not much wrong with it, rather a bad strip of the fabric ripped off as I was coming down, but I struck an abandoned farm yesterday a mile from here, and when I cover up the jigger, I'm just going over to see if I can fossick out something to patch her up."

"I guess I know where your strip of fabric is," I said.

I then told him of the white mark on the tree and how it led me to him, and as we went to salvage it, he told me of the mighty doings of the war.

"Let me see," he said, "you went out on your Zep. raid last February? Well, lots have happened since.

"Shortly after that Germany started to blockade England with submarines to starve her out, and began to sink all sorts of ships. They bagged a fine and large lot including some Americans—just sunk 'em on sight, asking no questions."

"Did America buck up, Nap?" I asked.

"Don't ask me, Jefson—that's the sick part. I want to dodge that. Let me get on—where was I? Oh, yes, Germany's submarine piracy; but that didn't do much harm, and she got tired of that stunt after a month or so. Then her fleet came out of Kiel to make a grand attack: at least, a bit of it came out, but only a bit of that bit got back again.

"Turkey, in the meantime had butted in and went for the Suez Canal, but your Australian fellows, who had been dropped at Egypt, made those bucks hike back quick and lively, then your Australians helped to chase them off the banks of the Dardanelles: and the British and French Fleets, smashing their way through, had threatened Constantinople—and then Turkey got the axe.

"All through February, March and April, Belgians, British and French held that line from Ostend to Nancy, getting a trench to-day and losing it to-morrow, all the while Kitchener was waiting for the winter to break and the Spring to come along and dry the roads for the cavalry and the big guns.

"In the east the Russian Army was just sitting like a rock. The Germans, relying on their idea of attack, were simply chucking themselves away on that Russian rock and smashing up like spray.

"Kitchener had six great armies waiting, but during May, June and July those armies doubled! The French and Russian Armies also practically doubled and streams increased from Australia and Canada.

"It was the most extraordinary thing of the war—and a young woman did it!

"She is a Belgian. She saw her mother being outraged by a German soldier. She slipped in, took up his bayonet, and skewered him, shot his companion, and with the weapon escaped to France. Through France and England she preached a crusade of Revenge. Crowds came to hear the sweet-faced woman speak frankly of unprintable horrors, and the fire of her tongue as she preached in her simple country dress with the bloodstained bayonet in her hand, won thousands of recruits. On top of her crusade out came the official report, that among other awful things, over 4000 Belgian women who had been maltreated by German soldiers would become mothers this year. Men with memories of dear mothers and sweet sisters tumbled over one another to hear and bless the world's new Joan of Arc, and marched in hundreds to recruiting stations with a fearful song of Revenge.

"Then she went to Italy! and though she spoke in a foreign tongue, the crowds understood and the Italians, passionate to the extreme, rose in storm—and Italy declared war!

"Italy got busy early in June, invading the Tyrol and smashing Pola on the Adriatic. Then its armies worked north, finding the great Austrian fortresses abandoned and destroyed, the big guns having been removed to be used against the Russians.

"Greece, when it found that Turkey was in danger of being smashed, joined with the Allies. It hung fire for a bit as its king was a relative of the Kaiser, but the people got sore, and at an election sent a popular Premier in who got the Greeks into the firing line.

"The principal Balkan States are also joining in the rumpus, as I guess they're anxious to be in the "top dog" so as to get some pickings after the scrap. Then in August we got the tip to get the big move on."

CHAPTER XVII.

How the Great War Ended.

I remember how Nap sparked up as he described the happenings of the past fortnight.

"We got the tip to prepare for the 'Grand Advance,'" he said. "Our stunt was to thoroughly screen from German aerial reconnaissance all our movements between Rheims and Metz; and so for a week the air actually swarmed with our 'planes. Gee! but the smash-up of aircraft was awful. We lost quite a collection, but the Germans must have very few left. And the way we went about it was a caution! We had a real aerial fandango—smashing bridges, trains, railway stations and any old thing. You see our commandants untied us —let us loose. Why one of my 'goes' was the bust up of the big balloon and 'plane 'deepo' at Laon; but in chasing a Taube three days ago I came to grief right here—engine trouble, sure."

"But what was the game, Nap?" I asked excitedly. "What was the reason of your aerial razzle?"

"Simple enough, Jefson," he replied, "we were screening a big transfer of our forces towards Metz. You see, the Germans, during June and July, had been pushed back to a line along the Lys, where they dug in on the right bank and waited.

"The great new armies Kitchener had in training during the winter were to be flung at that German line between Courtrai and Antwerp, to try and force their way through Belgium to Liege.

"We on the south were to put up a big bluff between Rheims and Metz in order to divert German attention from that big smashing attack on the Lys. Gee! How I'm itching to be back before the game starts!"

Then it all came back to me; the incident of the impatient German soldiers at the ferry on the Rhine; the tramp-tramp, rattle-clink of the German troops and carts on the Coblenz road; the anger of the little German woman at the farm— and one line of reasoning linked all the incidents.

"They've started," I said. "The Germans are retreating! That Coblenz road is a crowded procession of despair!"

He stopped and looked at me in surprise.

"How?" he queried. "Why we're 100 miles from Metz. Bless me, they must have started just after I lit out. Gee! but we must hustle."

So we stepped out briskly and reached the white strip on the tree. It was the piece of fabric from Nap's 'plane. That night we repaired the machine, and after many hours coaxed the engine back to sanity. Before the dawn the leafy screen was cleared, the 'plane wheeled into the open, the engine coughed, spluttered and "got busy"; and up to greet the morning sun we rose and turned southward with the sky clear of cloud, fog or 'plane.

As we climbed, we could discern the Coblenz road and the River Moselle below us, the former still a long length of moving figures. In half an hour, up came the sounds of big guns. Far to the south the opposing armies were evidently in touch. It was round Metz that the fighting was taking place, and we could see the "grey coats" retreating along at least five roads.

As we passed over Metz, I remembered my last crossing it in a fog and my dash to the Argonne Forest seven months before. Things had changed somewhat since.

We crossed the fighting lines and were lucky to descend without being hit, as several shots were fired as we volplaned down.

I remember, in those excitement-laden days, how for a while I was surprised that we were only welcomed back with a nod. There were evidently more important happenings to consider than the return of two lucky aviators, so we were soon again in operation with our squadron reconnoitring on our right to watch for any German reinforcements coming against our right flank.

It was evident that the Germans understood that our attack from the south was only a feint, as our advance was poorly retarded; in fact the German rearguard defence was so weak that our mounted forces began to push ahead rather quickly. The enemy was evidently concentrating on the Lys to oppose the Allies' main attack in West Belgium.

I remember that our forces to the left of Metz, the left wing of the southern armies, found an opening in the enemy's line at the Argonne Forest, and poured through: and being mostly French, Italian and Australian mounted troops, with artillery; speedily moved ahead, dashed into the Ardennes; and, being reinforced with our Metz forces joining them at Longwy, pushed on with a six road front through the Ardennes Forest. They concentrated in force at the edge of the forest on the left bank of the Lesse River to wait for the engineers.

Oh, what a mad dash that was! There seemed to be no thought of taking prisoners. It was a wild rush north, with, of course, every precaution taken for providing defence on both sides of our advance.

I remember that I wondered, at the time, why the Germans were almost without horses. Their dash across Belgium in the previous year explained the mobs of broken-backed, split-heeled and fleshless wrecks we met in the paddocks along the Meuse.

Within four days we occupied the whole of the country south of the Lesse River; with two railways, one a double line, feeding us with reinforcements and supplies.

Then our second dash began, and within a week our front was entrenched at the junction of the Meuse and Ourthe, with our artillery banging into the swarms of German infantry pouring into Liege!

What a sacrilege it seems to tell of this wonderful week in plain matter-of-fact language!

A week of feverish excitement, when one hardly remembered meals, sleep or rest, when our spirits raced in front of us pulling our responsive flesh!

I remember that when the French mounted troops, who led the way, lined the ridge beyond Nandrin and looked down upon the City of Liege between the hills they fairly screamed in their frenzied delight.

The main attack of the Allies had changed from the west to the south!

In the meantime our forces on our right extended along the Ourthe, with those on our left along the Meuse, two natural defensive positions, as the troops kept pouring in from the south to strengthen our attack.

We were as a spear-head at the heart of Germany, and great armies of French reinforcements were coming up behind us to drive that spear-head home!

Against that "spear-head" German reinforcements drawn from the eastern army flung themselves, but their attacks seemed spiritless. Russia had already broken their power.

Beneath a fearful fire from the Liege forts the Allies' armies poured across the Ourthe, climbed like cats on to the 200 foot ridge to the east of Liege; and within ten days all supplies for the German armies in Belgium were cut off!

On the second day of September, the main German armies in Belgium, that had held the line at the Lys, retired to their second line of defence at the Dendre, but almost before they could deploy the British were upon them and they unconditionally surrendered.

Thousands had fled to the Meuse, where the relentless French shells plowed passages through their ranks. Thousands had rushed, demoralised, northward, to be rounded up like wild cattle by the Dutch troops at the border line.

Then the British armies marched through Brussels and across the battle-blackened country easterly through Louvain; and at Liege joined hands with the armies from the south, as news came of the surrender of the German armies of the east.

The armies of Russia and Italy had been closing in on Vienna from the north and south.

Germany having no desire to get upon its own soil the awful devastation it had bestowed upon Belgium and France, through President Wilson, of the United States of America, asked the Allies for the terms of peace.

Then ensued a rather interesting situation.

The United States had not acted through the war with any admiration from the Allies.

Even when the German submarines had sunk the "Lusitania" and drowned over 1000 Americans, President Wilson did not take any action beyond practically asking Germany to frame any "old excuse." He was a man of peace. He seemed to have forgotten that the foundations of the U.S.A. were carved with a sword, and that Jefferson's first draft of the Declaration of Independence was militant and resistant. "For the support of this declaration," he wrote, "we mutually pledge our lives, our fortunes and our sacred honor."

President Wilson had previously informed the Allies that he was "too proud to fight," so when the message requesting the terms of peace came through Wilson, the Allies received it in a cold and formal fashion.

There are some phrases in the world's history that will live for ever. There is Kitchener's reply to General Cronje in the Boer War: "Not a minute"—there is Nelson's immortal message on the "Victory" of "England expects——"; so the reply of the Allies to America will long endure:—

"They who conquer can dictate the terms of peace."

Next day Germany and Austria pleaded for cessation of war.

Within fifteen months a world's war had begun and ended, and the events at its close had moved as swiftly as those at its beginning.

CHAPTER XVIII.

A Campaign of Errors.

So the Great War had ended.

In fifteen months the greatest tragedy the world had ever known came and passed. One could now calmly review the awful affair with an unbiassed mind. When one studied events during the war, there was always a prejudice against the enemy. His virtues were only "accidents" or strokes of luck. Our successes were always "brilliant affairs."

Yet the Great War was a campaign of blunders.

Victor Hugo said: "Alexander blundered in India, Cæsar blundered in Africa, Napoleon blundered in Russia."

After all, every book of war is a catalogue of errors, and the errors in a campaign, though unrealised at the time by those who make them, became palpable after the deed is done, and increase in notoriety as time passes.

British, French and German Generals blundered through the Great War. Only one nation came out of that awful clash of arms without criticism. It was Belgium.

The war opened with two mistakes on the part of Germany.

The first and greatest, as it proved now she was defeated, was the mistake of entering on a campaign that ended in her disaster.

Germany's second mistake was that of using heavy assaulting columns to charge the Liege forts, with the resultant horrible carnage. It was the old military rule of thumb. It went out at Liege, and the Mars of old, with his blood-dripping sword, had to stand aside as Modern Science stepped out of the Krupp factory with the great 42 centimeter gun. It took thirty horses to drag the first of these monsters out of that nest of the Prussian war eagle, and soldiers had to give way for that great weapon as it was drawn into place, accompanied by its retinue of mechanics and engineers, who set it up, armed, and fired it.

The monster required a concrete base; and concrete took 14 days to harden, but the Krupp experts brought a new concrete that hardened in 24 hours, and, within a week from leaving its home, the great Krupp demon began to batter a road through Liege.

France made the third blunder of the war as Belgium bravely held the gate at

Liege and awaited aid from France and England.

France, mistaking the main line of the German advance, massed the main army of her forces along the upper Meuse from Belfort, two hundred miles away from the right position.

Britain's first blunder was in not being prepared to immediately help Belgium. So the Krupp monsters smashed that Belgian gate and the German hordes swept towards Paris.

Britain somewhat retrieved her delay by quickly rushing to block the triumphant tide of Germany. And two British army corps saved the war by holding up five of Germany's best armies at Mons; holding them whilst they waited for the French to move up from their first mistakenly-held position; till, finding that aid not forthcoming, they fought back to the Marne.

Germany now blundered once again. Its aerial scouts failed to see a great French army coming at its right flank; failed to note it, because it came so swiftly out from behind Paris. It drove the German right towards its centre, past the British forces, which, catching the Germans on their flank, smashed them back to the readied trenches on the Aisne Ridge.

Then the Germans came round the north of Belgium, and Britain blundered again in sending a force of marines and reserves to hold Antwerp. They had to ignominiously retire as they found the country too flat for offensive manœuvring, and they had arrived too late to do the necessary extensive trenching which really meant the making of artificial land contours. That British force, however, helped to cover the retreat of the Belgian army.

Germany's final mistake was holding their position on the ridge of the Aisne. It could not have retreated without fearful loss as that ridge was the last conformation of any military value in the practically flat country between the Aisne and Liege.

After the war, experts maintained that it would, for many reasons, have been better strategy for Germany not to have crossed the Meuse in the first place.

The Germans were fired with the false idea that the capture of Paris meant the end of French aggression.

They had forgotten the lesson they learnt in 1870, when the capture of Paris did not end that campaign. They had forgotten the lessons of the Boer War, that the capture of the South African capitals did not terminate that long struggle.

They had their fixed plan. It had been prepared many years before and been put away till required, though military strategy had moved along in the meantime. At the first blast of war they blindly threw themselves across Belgium with their battle cry of 34 years before: "A Paris."

They could have occupied the country to the east of the Meuse, fortified the long length of high cliffs along its right bank, and sat there like a rock, letting the Allies smash themselves against it, whilst vast armies could have been free to push the Russians back to St. Petersburg, obtain supplies from Russia and so neutralise any British blockade.

Furthermore, having the fight nearer German soil would have given the German people a better idea of the actual state of the war and helped to stifle any lack of enthusiasm on the part of German Socialists which, later on, was to develop into serious trouble.

It was a war of surprises.

Science had laid its new-won gifts at the feet of Mars.

It brought as new factors into human warfare, wireless telegraphy, aeronautics and motor traction.

Wireless telegraphy, one of the greatest gifts to mankind in the saving of human life at sea, and in the sending of messages of peace, utterly failed during the stress of human strife.

It seemed that just as clashing human passions in war stultified all thoughts of brotherly love and goodwill, so the ether waves from military wireless plants clashed in the air and destroyed all intelligence in messages.

In aeronautics, the swift aeroplane asserted its superiority over the balloon, and where movements were in open country as between Liege and the Aisne, it furnished a new and wonderful aid for reconnaissance.

It failed when the movements took place beneath cover, as in the fighting in the thickly wooded country to the south of Compeigne; again, when the French army moved out under cover of the houses of Paris and environs before the battle of Marne; and finally when, in the conclusive phases of the war the Allies moved north beneath the screen of the forests of the Argonne and the Ardennes.

Motor traction counted most in the new aids of science. It brought into the war the most vital factor of all human element—speed.

The great smash on the German right at the Marne, which gave the first check to the German advance, was only possible because the French General, Gallieni, moved 70,000 soldiers out of Paris in taxicabs and other motor vehicles, and in six hours had them in action before even the German aerial reconnaissance knew about it.

The motor brought speed into the fighting in running the cheering soldiers to the front, and with auto hospitals brought the sorry wounded as speedily back again.

It was a triumph for the machine, and yet the machine, in the end, gave place to the hand to hand death grip of primitive man.

As Kipling wrote:—

"What I ha' seen since ocean steam began
Leaves me no doot for the machine; what, what about the man?"

The Great War answered that question.

There was a doubt about the man—he dropped off the veneer of the human and became the animal once again.

When foe came face to face with foe the world dropped back ten thousand years.

CHAPTER XIX.

The Revolution.

And now the war was over—bar the shouting.

I remember the soldiers had strange emotions at the sudden ending to fifteen months' activity. At times they would be excited, and at others disappointed. It seemed like the feeling of the London 'busman who left off work for a week's holiday, but found himself on a 'bus next day asking the driver to "let him hold the ribbons for a bit."

The war fever had got into our blood, and the camps, instead of being orderly in arrangement, became moving masses of wandering soldiers. Discipline snapped as the news of Peace passed through the ranks. Some soldiers would cheer—they had loved ones awaiting their return. Others took it as a matter of little concern—they, no doubt, had cut all ties in enlisting, and, perhaps, wondered if their old places had been kept open for them.

Troops still poured in from the south, adding to the demoralisation.

I remember that the commandant of my air corps rose with me in the 'plane and surveyed the wonderful scene.

Around Liege troops were moving in a wonderful mass, not unlike the mixed crowd that one sees in a city street after a procession has passed along, but with the crowd increased a thousandfold.

Yet it was not a disorderly crowd. It seemed a crowd of good fellowship. The German soldiers in the west had fought against the British and found them brave enemies. The revulsion of feeling made them friends. The tension of hate snapped.

It has ever been thus. With a quarrel over, the greatest haters become the warmest friends.

For two days the armies at the Meuse fraternised.

Our soldiers learnt much from their former enemies. They found, through some papers that had slipped the eyes of the censors, that the Socialists of Germany were in revolt.

I could then understand the excitement of my religious friend, Brother Wilbrid, on the Rhine road, and his anxiety to get back to Berlin without loss of time.

It appears that the first public indication of the insurrection took place as far back as December 2, 1915, when a party of fifteen Socialist deputies in the Reichstag, led by Karl Leibknecht, refused to vote for the second war credits. Four of these members were from Berlin. One, Stadthagen, represented a popular workmen's suburb in Berlin, while another, Geyer, represented a workers' suburb in Leipsic. The Socialists of Bremen, Stuttgart and Hamburg endorsed the Socialist Deputies' refusal by a majority of two to one. Not only were the Socialist party rising in revolt, but the Moderates, under Bernstein, were opposed, because the war was entered into by Socialists exclusively as a war against Russia, whilst the authorities had cleverly turned the reason as a war against England. Though the Socialists may have hated England, the war proved that they were used as a cat's paw. So riots broke out in Berlin, Stuttgart and Hamburg.

In Berlin, down the Unter der Linden, a mighty mob of workers marched and stoned the Government offices. The military police dispersed them.

Fate helped the revolt.

At the surrender of the German armies, thousands of German soldiers, rather than surrender, had retreated along the roads leading into Germany, sullenly shouting the news of the defeat.

Bad news travels fast, and to the German people, who had been kept in ignorance of reverses, the news came with stunning effect.

Only a few days before had the authorities at Berlin announced to the Socialists that ultimate success was certain, and bade the people be of good cheer. Now, like a crash, came the news of defeat with the additional disgrace of being brought by retreating soldiers of the Empire!

Then the revolution crashed on Germany. It was a riot that rolled round the earth.

I remember it was a week after our arrival at Liege that the armies of the Allies began their march to the Rhine. They had not yet reached German soil, and the Peace terms would not be disclosed till the Allies were in Germany.

To my delight, the French army of the Argonne was given the post of honor. It must have been a wonderful sight to see the Air Squadron of twelve aeroplanes moving backward and forward over the heads of the moving columns. Nap accompanied me in my 'plane, and I remember I kept somewhat in advance of the rest to catch the first sight of Cologne Cathedral.

It came upon the horizon, its two great spires piercing the sky unscathed. How unlike the Churches of Rheims, Ypres and the other cities of France and Belgium. Germany well knew the value of its historical buildings to protect them, even at the price of peace. We flew low to give a more spectacular effect to our advance.

Soon the great piers of the familiar Rhine Bridge came into sight as the order was given to descend on a plain to the west of the river.

That night the army bivouacked on the outskirts of Aix la Chappele, but sleep did not come to my eyes. At times I desired to fly ahead to Cologne and tread the familiar ways—but strict regulations tied all troops to the camp lines.

I comforted myself that to-morrow I would reach Cologne and someone would be pleased to see me.

Next day we crossed the Rhine, circled the city of Cologne, and parked our 'planes in the gardens I had left but three weeks previously.

The Allied troops were marched through the city and encamped two miles beyond it. A regiment of French soldiers were deputed as military police to take possession of the city; and within an hour, from the poles of the official buildings, French, Belgian, Russian and British flags fluttered, and an order was issued that all arms must be handed in.

I remember the happy feeling as Nap and I hastened through the city to Goche's house.

I was in my uniform and felt I would cut a smarter figure before my sweetheart, than I did in the ragged "cast-offs" I wore as a prisoner.

I walked on air when I entered the familiar street and saw, in the distance, the house I knew so well. The street was silent. I reached the house, pulled myself together and knocked at the door. Happiest of thoughts coursed through my mind. What a wealth of news I had to tell her!

The door slowly opened, and Grandpa Goche's whitened and aged face came to the light. His under jaw seemed to shiver in terror. He gave the impression that he was expecting some dreadful calamity. As he recognised me, his jaw fell and he retreated into the room, sank into a chair, gripped its arms with shaking clutch, looked at me with hollow eyes and said: "Ja wohl."

"Where is Helen?" I asked.

"Forgive me," he said, "forgive me," shaking his head. "They came to me and asked for the Englishman that escaped—'the English dog' they called you. I told them I knew not, but as I hated you and hated her, for I knew she cared for you, I told them she could tell, as she saw you leave. Then they took her," and he bowed his head in his hands, "took her away——"

"Where, where?" I almost shouted at him.

"To Berlin, a week ago," was all he said.

"In Berlin."

CHAPTER XX.

Footing the Bill.

It is difficult at this distant date to give in detail the story of the riot that began in Berlin and thundered round the earth toward the end of 1915.

While the Great War was under way the belligerents were like gamblers crowded round a table, as they threw down their millions in men and money to beat the whirling finger of Fate.

Great Britain and her Allies had 12,600,000 men and had spent £1,180,000,000. Germany, Austria and Turkey had 8,800,000 men and had spent £1,282,000,000. When the awful game was over there were over 18,000,000 people to go back to civil life, many of whom were crippled. Withal the belligerents had lost over £9,000,000,000 in direct expenditure, loss of production and capitalised value of the human sacrifice.

These 18,000,000 men were flung back into civil life at a time when almost all productive industry was crippled or paralysed. The world could not immediately reorganise her industries and taxation promised to be colossal.

When men came back to their homes, or what was left of them, took off their uniforms and put their guns behind the doors, they sat down and pondered. They began to count up the cost and wondered how to foot the bill.

One can, therefore, easily understand they did not form a high opinion of the wisdom of those who had governed them and exacted unquestioning obedience from them.

Was it any wonder then that they should consider they might as well take a hand in governing? They could not make a worse mess of things than those who claimed to have had a divine commission for the job. When the masses, who had furnished the bulk of the soldiers, began to think, the position became dangerous, especially as real thinking had stopped fifteen months before and there was a call for overtime in thinking to make up.

The man with the gun would remember that before Britain entered the war there was a heavy tax per head. He would find out that though Britain had been attempting to cheer herself up during the war with a motto of "Business as Usual," her exports had diminished by £50,000,000, and the actual cost had been £1,250,000,000!

Then he would think very hard.

If he were French he would remember that before the war opened France had a permanent debt of £1,269,223,600, or £32.05 for every man, woman and child.

If he were Russian he would remember that before the war the national debt was £1,461,000,000, with annual loss of revenue from the Vodka monopoly of £140,000,000.

If he were German he would remember that the war tax had been £74,700,000, and that the war had cost £2,770,000,000.

One question would come into the minds of those 18,000,000 thinkers. Who was going to pay for this loss of £9,000,000,000?

One answer came from Germany.

It was voiced by Wilbrid the Humanist.

The "psychological" had arrived for sounding the note of revolt. It was struck and echoed round the earth; even throughout America!

"Europe is filled with human wrecks," Wilbrid preached.

"All the time the physical stamina of Europe was being destroyed on the battlefield, national debts piled up, adding phenomenal burdens to the already crushing taxes cast on the toilers.

"Millions still unborn must toil the harder and live the meaner for every day of the monstrous lunacy.

"There is only one reason for the ocean of blood and tears.

"Eighty per cent. of the world's population belong to a class supported by its own exertions—the working class. It only gets back half the wealth it produces; the other half goes to the 20 per cent. that does not toil; but as that 20 per cent. cannot consume that half, markets must be found for what is over, and some nation must yield markets, colonies and dumping grounds to another nation able to put into the field stronger battalions and deadlier guns. Those conditions must be altered or this peace will be only an armed truce.

"War can be abolished by giving the 80 per cent. who produce the result of their efforts, instead of paying it to the 20 per cent.; in short, let all the results of labor go toward the Common Good.

"Men should work for humanity generally, not for an individual. That system would kill competition in manufacture between individuals and nations.

"All men should be prepared to fight for humanity, not for an individual. That would kill monarchy.

"The Great War debts can be paid by taxing those 20 per cent. non-workers who have been taking more than their share since time began.

"It is those non-workers that made the war by their competition for trade, for individual power and personal wealth. So let them pay for it.

"The age of individualism ended with the war. There will be no further need for that 'joke of the ages' at Hague. A 'Palace of Peace' erected by a 'millionaire'! No wonder the Hague conventions were 'scraps of paper.'"

It was such doctrines that brought about the revolution.

It was not a revolution of force, although at its outset a mob of irresponsibles stoned the Government offices in Berlin. The distinctive note preached by the Humanists was abolition of armed force and reform by constitutional means. So when Wilbrid's mighty "Army of Humanity" marched through Berlin as a demonstration of numbers, half of its ranks were soldiers. But they walked with arms reversed as a proof of the death of "Armed Force."

The presence of the soldiers in the crowd was evidently misunderstood at Potsdam, for that day the Kaiser and his staff fled and the Government resigned.

Then the wonderful organising ability of Brother Wilbrid asserted itself. Within a few days the socialistic doctrines of the Humanists covered Germany.

The doctrines found ready acceptance. The Humanists pointed out that their advocacy of the control of production by the Government for the Common Good was not so novel in its application.

They showed that, before the war, the railways were Government-owned, and it was ready to nationalise the electrical industry.

They showed that, during the war, every nation had taken over railway traction and was manufacturing and supplying to citizens certain necessaries of life.

They showed that in Britain for many years men who had argued that the Government should take over and operate the privately-owned railways were looked upon as revolutionaries, extremists and fanatics; yet on the very day war was declared the British Government reached out and seized every railroad and began to operate it.

"During the war Germany was manufacturing and supplying citizens with food, clothing and shelter," preached Wilbrid. "If Governments can do that for the sake of war they can do it for the sake of peace. If they can operate clothing factories to clothe soldiers, they can operate them to clothe citizens. If they can operate food factories to feed soldiers on the firing line, they can operate food factories to feed starving citizens. If such things can be done to destroy life, they can do these things to preserve it."

These fantastic phrases struck home.

The fact was that the masses foresaw colossal taxation following the war, and jumped at any opportunity of letting some one else pay it.

It was the old story of the "have-nots" and the "haves," with the result that the Reichstag became almost unanimously a Humanist assembly.

CHAPTER XXI.

Into Berlin.

It seemed strange at the time that the Allies' forces were being kept out of Berlin till the elections were decided. The wisdom of it was afterwards ascertained, however.

The allied armies were kept out of Berlin because their presence there would have given opportunity for tumult, and perhaps seriously interrupted the course of events the Humanists were, perhaps unconsciously, shaping in favor of the Allies.

The change in German politics cleared out the Hohenzollern regime, deposed the Kaiser and his class, and as the chief policy doctrine of the Humanists was disarmament, it suited the Allies to let the people do the work for them.

The wisdom of this step was evident when news came through that the Humanist movement was spreading across France and England.

In Belgium and France it met with more opposition than it did in Germany. Strange to say the Belgian "Joan of Arc" was the leader. She preached the cause of "the capitalist" with much vigor. I do not know why she took up this political campaign. Maybe the wonderful response to her appeals for financial aid for the starving Belgians won her sympathy when she saw the capitalistic class that helped her in danger of being destroyed.

Her eloquence, spiced by anecdote and parable, won many followers. She pointed out that the doctrine of the Humanist in abolishing world competition hit at the fundamental principle that made for initiative and made man utilise thought and self-improvement.

"Abolish competition or distinction," she said, "and all men come under the one rule, like so many animals."

She pointed to Joffre and Kitchener as successful examples of the old and well-tried system.

She pointed to Belgium's King, Albert, who fought throughout the war in the fighting line, sharing the lot of the soldier. She was joined in her campaign by many of her own sex, even from Berlin, whence many had departed, at the advent of the Humanist campaign which was spreading throughout Germany.

When the Reichstag elections were decided, a force from each of the Allied armies entrained for Berlin and, to my delight, my company was among those favored.

It is difficult for one accustomed to plain writing to tell in fitting phrases the wonderful enthusiasm that reigned as our troop-trains slowly rolled into Berlin.

Along ten lines, crowded with continuous trains, we were conveyed to our destination. Our trains were preceded by slow trains which dropped guards at each bridge and station.

As our train steamed into the depot outside Berlin, I saw the wonderful system of getting away troops. As soon as a train arrived columns poured into a great park adjoining and took up allotted places.

As we passed along the streets the populace did not show any of the fright and fear we fancied our presence would cause. They chatted, smiled and pointed at us as if it were an ordinary parade of troops and not the triumphant conquerors of their country.

Truth to tell, they were mighty sick of the war and the long preparation, and our presence proved it was all over.

I remember, best of all, the frenzied welcome we received from the Russian forces who had trained in from the south east.

They had kept the enemy busy on the east whilst we were moving up. It was like the meeting of many friends who had come through adversity together.

I can only picture one simile. I remember a story of two miners imprisoned in a mine. They were cut off from all help and separated, but began digging to meet one another. After many hours they cut through the wall of clay that stood between them. Their hand-grip must have been as ours was on that wonderful day in August.

It would take three days for all troops to detrain, so I sought the earliest opportunity of finding Miss Goche. Nap came with me. The only clue I had was that she had been removed to a concentration camp at Berlin. I found that camp. A military officer who could speak English saluted as we approached and informed us that all foreign military prisoners had been transferred to Belgium and given their liberty.

“Was a Miss Goche among them?” I anxiously asked.

“I cannot say,” he replied.

My heart sank. I felt that it was a difficult task for a stranger unacquainted with German and a former enemy to attempt to trace the information.

Nap tapped me on the shoulder, and in order to cheer me said: “You’ve got a friend here, come and look him up.”

There would be little difficulty in finding Wilbrid, he was now a public character. So we took a car for the Humanist headquarters and there we found him seated at a large desk in his shirt sleeves. On either side of him were two dictaphones, and into the cylinders he was alternatively dictating his correspondence. As one cylinder would fill it would automatically ring, and he would turn to the other, an assistant removing the filled cylinder.

We stood behind him at the end of the room afraid to interrupt, but he turned and, seeing me, rose and came with outstretched hand.

"My brother Jefson," he said. "I know your first desire. You have been to the concentration camp. I found your friend there. When I returned to Cologne I found she had been arrested for assisting your escape. I traced her to the camp, gave her your letter and saw much of her for your sake. But she has gone—to Belgium. She was high-spirited. I talked much to her of the Humanist creed, but she would have none of it: so on her release she left for Belgium and she joined the woman called the Belgian "Joan of Arc."

CHAPTER XXII.

The Great Combine.

"Your war has ended at last," said Wilbrid, after a long pause. "Ours is but beginning; and our conquest will not be limited by an empire's boundaries, or even by those of a continent. It will embrace the earth." Having spoken he turned to the window and peered at the blood-red sunset contemplatively.

I surveyed his tall, spare figure, his steel grey hair and sharply-cut features, the latter pinked by the evening glow.

Here is a new Kaiser, I thought.

"You said a 'world conquest,'" I remarked to him. "Don't you think the days have gone when persons should 'talk big'? The great war should henceforth limit the ambitions of those who dream of world's dominion by conquest."

"Do not misunderstand me," he said. "We shall conquer the world because of the human appeal of our creed. Its basis is that the strength of a nation lies in the welfare of its producers—the working class, and not in its mighty armaments or individual wealth. There is not an atom of national strength in the accumulation of much money by any individual. Where wealth is in the hands of the few, misery stalks among the many; and, where the masses are ill-fed and hopeless, moral and physical strength cannot exist."

Then he walked from the window to his desk and back again; his arms still behind him, flinging his phrases at us as he passed to and fro.

"Great things can only be achieved by combination," he went on. "The victory of the Allies is proof of that. We are going to combine all workers, and, in order to make our combination supreme, we will not only organise those at work, but, also, those out of work. It is going to be a combination of all who can labor," he snapped out.

"Up till now," he continued, "there have been more men in the world than there have been jobs to go round; so there have always been many unemployed. Those unemployed are the men who keep down the wages of the workers. If there were no men or women to take the jobs from those who work, then the workers could demand shorter hours and a better share of the wealth they produce. It is the unemployed who have been keeping up the competition in wages. That is where they have been useful to the employer.

"Up till now the workers have struggled to hold their jobs; and have fought to maintain or raise their wages without taking into account the thousands of unemployed who need work.

"Those out of work are humans after all, and when hunger drives them to take the work at lower wages, they're called 'scabs' and other vile names; and we have treated them as our bitterest enemies.

"Can you blame a man whose wife is sinking and whose children cry for food, if he is willing to take a job at less than the wage you get?

"Would not any man lower the wages scale and take another man's job for less, in order to save the life of his wife and the new baby? Should any union principles stand between him and his wife's life? That is why we are going to combine with the unemployed."

It had grown dark, so he stepped to the wall and touched a switch. As the light flooded the room I ventured a reply.

"Don't you think the human appeal in your creed is rather one-sided," I remarked. "Why not purge your workers' unions first! You know there are certain trade unions that make the entrance fees so high, that many of their own trade are excluded."

"There is a Wharf Laborers' Union in Australia that has an entrance fee that is considered to prohibit new membership, and it has as its secretary a Federal Minister of the Crown."

"I guess you're right just there," Nap put in. "The Union of Glass Blowers of the U.S.A. demand 1000 dollars as initiation fee; so they get fine pay and they're 'some' people, I guess."

"There are unions in Australia," I rejoined, "that not only demand a high entrance fee, but, in order to continue a monopoly of employment, are limiting the number of apprentices who desire to learn their trade.

"There are unionists who, when work is slack and members are unemployed, will advocate shorter hours at the same rate of pay so as to make room for their unemployed mates.

"And, perhaps, you are not aware that Australia is a land where Nature is so generous that in its short history it has reached the highest level in the world's wheat and wool production. Yet in that land, twenty times the size of your Germany and with one-thirteenth of your population, the workers discourage immigration of people of their own British race, because they foolishly fancy the newcomers would create competition in their high-priced work; and that is in a wonderful land crying out for development and only having an average population of one person to the square mile."

I finished in a highly-strung manner, but Wilbrid came forward and put his hands on my shoulders.

"My boy," he said calmly, "you are right, and I am also right. That selfishness on the part of the workers is but the fear of having their wages cut and becoming unemployed with the advent of further competition. Remove that fear and keep the unemployed from cutting wages and the selfishness will disappear. The Humanist creed recognises all men as sparks of Divinity. There will be no 'scabs,' 'pimps,' 'blacklegs,' or other vile, cruel epithets. The men and women who work will combine with those unemployed. The result will be such a world's combination of labor that all sources of profit-winning will be in the hands of the men who toil. It will indeed be a conquest of the world.

"Already we control the Governments of Germany and Austria. France and England will certainly follow at the next elections. The French workers do not forget that, during the war, their Government successfully organised the whole of the industries; and the English toilers remember how the Asquith Government successfully controlled all the great munition factories and limited the employers' profits to 10 per cent., giving the surplusage to the State. Now I note that the British workers are demanding that just as the State successfully controlled great works during the war and claimed the profits in excess, so it should control all works now and let the profits go also to the Common Good—yes, that's the term. It's almost a divine inspiration. The Common Good is the doctrine of the Humanist! Watch the cause! It will sweep the earth!"

As he shook hands with me, I could feel his nerves twitching.

Nap and I walked back to the great camp almost in silence, and little sleep came to me that night.

CHAPTER XXIII.

The Terms of Peace.

I shall never forget the grand march of the Allies through Berlin, and the sealing of the Treaty of Peace.

There had been much delay regarding what the Terms of Peace should be. Great Britain was the stumbling block.

Eighty years before, Washington Irving wrote of "John Bull":—

> "Though no one fights with more obstinacy to carry a contested point, yet when the battle is over and he comes to reconciliation, he is so much taken up with the mere shaking of hands, that he is apt to let his antagonists pocket all they have been fighting about."

England proved that once again in South Africa, for after fighting five years with the Boers, she actually gave them what they were fighting for—their independence.

With Germany she was inclined to be generous, but the French, Belgian and Russian delegates urged firmness, and the Terms of Peace were finally settled.

It was estimated that the actual expenditure of the Allies was £1,180,000,000, and the loss in shipping £250,000,000, a total loss of £1,430,000,000.

Germany and Austria had to hand over to the Allies the whole of their Navies to be held for the protection of the world's peace, and each nation had to pay an indemnity of £1,000,000,000. The German prisoners had to be kept in Belgium for nine months to repair damage done to Belgian towns. The boundaries of France and Belgium were to be extended to the Rhine. Holland was to be absorbed by a joint protectorate that took in the Schleswig-Holstein Peninsula. Poland was to go back to Russia, Servia and Italy being allotted the shorelines of the Adriatic. The Dardanelles was to be an open, undefended waterway. Bulgaria was to absorb Turkey in Europe, Russia obtaining further concessions in Caucasia.

There were other details of the terms that need not be here mentioned. But on the 1st day of December, 1915, the Treaty of Berlin confirmed them.

There was little demonstration in Germany. The new political party in power, the Humanists, had already agreed to disarmament; so the first part of the treaty did not trouble. The policy of "universal brotherhood" subdued any qualms that might have arisen regarding loss of territory. Regarding the indemnity: it could be met by imposing a heavy income tax on all incomes over 3000 marks (£150). By this means the Humanists would make the capitalists pay for the war.

The Humanist Government readily accepted the demand of the Allies that the German prisoners should not be returned to Germany for nine months. They were drafted into great work-camps in Belgium, and were put to replacing bridges, reconstructing buildings, and making good all they had devastated.

I remember at the time, how the world jeered at the so-called "Humanist" Government in Germany, because it so readily agreed to the harsh treatment of the "Sons who fought for the German Empire." But the Berlin officials were wise. For nine months an army of 800,000 men were being fed and kept at the Allies' expense. That mob was thus prevented from returning to an overstocked manufacturing nation. They were being held back to give their country nine months' opportunity to "put its house in order."

CHAPTER XXIV.

What Happened in England.

On leaving Berlin our squadron was part of the force that had to return to England. I had hoped to break the journey at Brussels, to meet Helen Goche, but Fate stepped in. To my disappointment the troop-trains passed on to Ostend along a line to the south of Brussels.

On arrival in England, the Flying Corps were not disbanded, but were attached to the permanent forces.

Nap, however, desired to return to the United States, and as we shook hands in "good-bye," I felt I was losing a friend to whom adventurous days had linked me by heart-grips.

"I'm going along through to that country of yours," he said to me as he swung into the train. "From what you tell me, it must be 'some place.' We'll grip again there, sure." And the train pulled out and tore him out of my life for many days.

The months succeeding the Declaration of Peace were troublesome times for England. Troops were pouring back from the Continent and being dismissed to return to jobs they found had disappeared.

During the war a fine spirit of "cheer up" generally prevailed. People tried to put vim into themselves by tacking the motto over their shops: "Business as Usual." They knew full well that business was nearly dead; but they were like the boy who whistled going through the graveyard in order to keep up his courage.

Apart from the trades making munitions of war, few factories maintained their full output. Recruiting lessened the number of employees, and those who stayed behind fought for shorter hours and higher wages. Investors generally eased off, as money was too high in value to risk in new concerns in such uncertain times. Even the highly boosted scheme to bring back to England from Germany the Aniline dye industry failed for the want of the necessary capital.

Then a great movement was inaugurated throughout the British Empire. "Trade only with the Allies." It seemed a fine idea in theory, but when Russia, in desiring to place an order for £1,400,000 worth of railway plant, found English prices inflated by labor demands and placed the order with America, the "Trade-only-with-the-Allies" movement began to wobble.

Then the troops began to pour back into England in thousands. Manufacturers and investors kept off of any new enterprises as they saw the Asquith Government, always rather radical, lending a sympathetic ear to the workers' demand that the State should control all industries.

Cities and towns now began to fill with unemployed and riots broke out everywhere.

Then the Government took action. All steel and woollen industries were placed under military control with "preference to returned soldiers."

The outcries of the owners were pacified by the promise of 10 per cent. of all profits on work done, with proportional profits according to the value of the plant and enterprise. But under the military control, as increased wages were given and shorter hours worked in order to absorb all unemployed, profits diminished rapidly.

The General Elections in February, 1916, divided the country into two parties. The Humanist party, headed by Lloyd-George and Blatchford, aiming at Government control of all production, and the Individualist party, in which Winston Churchill was prominent, standing for "private enterprise." Though the latter had behind it the full force of British capitalists, the Humanist party, elected on a general franchise, swept the poll. Thus England became Socialistic. Heavy land and income taxes followed with high wages ruling for the working classes. It was a bloodless revolution!

CHAPTER XXV.

Belgium Holds the Gate Again.

It was shortly after the Humanist Government assembled in London that considerable disbandment in the British military forces took place, my squadron, amongst others, being marked out. I lost no time in crossing to Brussels. I remember when I again met Helen Goche I felt, at first, a strange reserve, fearing that our short friendship in Cologne had no deeper meaning for her; but we both realised that henceforward our paths would be together; so I joined her in her work with the Belgian "Joan of Arc."

I never knew the name of this wonderful woman. We simply called her "Madame"; but her power of organising was remarkable and recalled to my mind the similar success of Wilbrid in Germany.

Madame was the head of an organisation that had a branch in every town in Belgium.

Tall and somewhat thin, without any striking personal beauty, she stood erect before her audience, and, with the sincerity of her purpose, carried all before her.

The second night of my return, I went with Helen to a great assembly where, for two hours, ten thousand Belgians absorbed the purpose of her phrases.

"Men of Belgium," she said, "we are asked, in these days of peace, to forget and forgive; but can you ever forget those terrible days of 'frightfulness' the German swine inflicted upon us and our beloved country?

"Return to your homes, your farms and your factories, but take with you a hate for the Huns—a hate that time can never heal. To forgive may be divine, but justice is the prime attribute to divinity. Justice in this case calls for our undying hate. And now these Germans, not content with having tried to subjugate our flesh, are trying to subjugate our minds and our very souls. Think well upon the tempting creed of the Humanists that was 'Made in Germany.'

"It is a creed that calls for State control of all production; a creed that cuts out all private enterprise and initiative; a creed that forces men to shut down upon their self-development and independence and to rely upon employment by the State.

"I ask you, men of Belgium, to look at those whom the State employs to-day. Eight hundred thousand Germans are under State control to make good the works they have wantonly destroyed. They may repair the bridges and the highways, but there are broken hearts they cannot heal, and—there are many empty chairs in Belgian homes.

"Do any of you wish to have the brand of shame those wastrels wear? Do any of you wish to have broken that national independent spirit that made our brothers bravely hold the Gate at Liege?

"To-day this German-made Humanist creed has gripped Germany, England, France and Austria. It stands for the levelling of the human being. None can rise above the common level. They call it the gospel of the Common Good, but there is nothing good in anything that clips the wings of those who would dare to excel; that baulks the aspirations of those who would use the brains their God has given them that they may rise.

"I tell you this 'Humanist' creed, rating all men as equal, and only recognising each man and each woman as one in a mob of similar animals, will lower the race till even your name will be replaced with a numeral. It is a creed akin to the German ideal of the man-animal that dragged a bloody trail across our country.

"I tell you, the creed must fail that cannot recognise any degrees of mental capacity; that cannot understand that man has a soul that cannot be confined within any man-drawn boundaries. This German-creed sweeps the earth with all the bombast of a war-mad Kaiser. It is going to fail, but not till men who think will rise and fight for recognition of their immortality. It will be the War of the Ages!

"And in the fight Belgium will stand firm once again as the Buffer State of Civilisation. It will hold the gate for the future of Humanity."

I came away from that meeting impressed with the air of prophecy in the discourse, for Belgium was standing firm for Individualism. A lonely State in a developing world of Socialism, and though Kings in other lands began to fear the safety of their crowns, Albert of Belgium was still the beloved sovereign of a prosperous people.

It was strange how Belgium quickly recovered from the war!

The energy generated by that conflict, the confidence engendered by success, and the adaptability and resourcefulness taught by the war, set off the loss of many of her manhood.

The war was a forerunner of a vigorous period of expansion of Belgian industry, for the employment of 800,000 German prisoners on national works set free the population to develop various enterprises.

Another incentive to excel was the practical sympathy the world had shown to Belgium in her days of distress. It put such stimulation into the nation that it felt it had to make good to merit the world's high regards.

I write at length on this remarkable sequel to the war on the part of Belgium, as other nations did not rise to the occasion like it did. The Socialistic doctrines of the Humanist countries sapped at the initiative of the worker, advanced his wages, but crushed the men of wealth and forced them to seek new fields for their enterprise.

It is a trait of the human nature that he, desiring to excel, will eventually rise; so the men of enterprise, the men of initiative, the men who do things, came to Belgium though many sought wider fields of enterprise across the seas.

CHAPTER XXVI.

What a Letter from Australia Told Me.

Australia had sent 100,000 men to the front at a cost of £18,000,000, which was covered by a loan from Britain.

Though the decline in trade on account of the war caused widespread unemployment, the sending off of 75,000 men eased matters considerably. As these men were paid at almost the same rate as their ordinary wage, and as a big proportion of their pay was held in Australia, the war did not hit the Commonwealth so very hard in this respect.

So people did not trouble much. They went about their business almost as usual and enjoyed the many entertainments arranged by "society people" for any object, however remotely connected with the war—"Sheepskin Waistcoat Funds," "Comfort for Horses Fund," "Knitted Socks Fund," and others. It was all so much work and gave people opportunity to have a busy time, flavored with the knowledge that it was an act of patriotism.

Six months before the war had ended the manufacturers began to get busy. When public bodies begin to get busy in Australia, the first thing they say is: "Let's have a Dinner."

The manufacturers saw a chance of influencing High Protection by the use of a new gag: "Don't buy German-made goods." They, of course, wanted people to buy only the Australian made, but they were cute.

They put it this way:

"Only trade with the Empire and its Allies. Every pound," it was said, "that is spent with Germany means another gun to our future menace." So the public were exhorted to confine business to the Empire and its Allies—with Britain, Africa, India, Canada, France, Belgium, Russia, Servia and Japan, and to cut the rest of the world. That is to say, to trade with three quarters of the world!

Their decision practically meant free trade with nearly the whole world, and so their hands were tied so long as Britain was joined up with foreign allies!

A striking proof that this slogan, "Trade with the Allies," was only an after-dinner sentiment was given when, in May, 1915, the Australian Postmaster-General rejected a Japanese tender for electric insulators, although its price was £1000 cheaper than a local tender, the total amount of which was £3281/6/8—a thirty-three per cent. preference being given against the work of an allied nation.

In the meantime the N.S.W. Government found their system of State Socialism so expensive that the Treasury began to rapidly empty. The war, with its upsetting of the British money market, stopped the usual method of loan-raising, but some smart English capitalists, more experienced in finance than the average labor politician, offered to take over the public works of New South Wales if they were paid 10 per cent. on their expenditure.

They 'cutely pointed out that by the system of State Socialism, the N.S.W. Government had gathered an immense army of laborers. It had built up an enormous civil service, and if men were thrown on the market consequent on the State's lack of funds, they would make it uncomfortable for the Government. That action would bring home to the workers the utter fallacy of State control of industries. They also whispered, with their tongues in their cheeks, that "private enterprise" would then become prosperous and the Labor movement would be thrown back for "years and years and years."

The temptation proved too strong and the compact was signed.

"Of course," said the Government, "you will give preference to unionists, the maximum wage, and all that?"

"Oh, of course," said the Syndicate, rubbing its hands with glee.

It was getting 10 per cent. on all the expenditure!

What though the men loafed through the work, the percentage of the outlay went on just the same!

So the N.S.W. Government signed the compact, practically threw over State Socialism, so far as public works were concerned, thanked goodness for the riddance, and sat back for a while, stripped of responsibility, a Syndicate's collection of "rubber stamps."

Some of the Ministers, however, tired of the "nothin'-doin' policy," hankered after the tinpot glory they had when in charge of men, so they began to look for new fields of enterprise not touched by the Syndicate.

They saw an opportunity in Government bread-making.

The Government had heard a good deal about the profit possibilities of great American "combines." Why not introduce the thing into Australia as a great Government scheme, and combine all the small bakery establishments into one big concern, in which great automatic baking machinery would supplant the small ovens of the small employers?

This would not only knock out the "hated employers," but it would capture all their profits—and the Government wanted money rather badly.

So, immense bread-making factories were built. A standard price was put on wheat the Government wanted, which knocked the farmer rather hard and hundreds of employees were thrown out of the bakehouses.

It was an awkward situation for a Government pledged to Socialism. The unionists had shouted for Socialism, yet when Socialism brought in labor-saving machines, when, in fact, it hit the chap who shouted, he objected. Socialism seemed alright "for the other fellow." It was like the old story of the Irishman's pigs. He believed in sharing alike, except regarding pigs—he happened to have a few.

The Socialist Government was in a quandary with its mob of unemployed baker unionists, till the voice of the tempter came again.

The Syndicate quietly whispered, "Give us a little more power and we'll absorb them."

They got it, and got further power as the Government installed labor-saving machinery into other concerns; and for a while the Syndicate proved a fine "haven of rest" for the out-of-work unionists, so that the Government encouraged it even to the extent of absolving it from having to pay income tax.

"You see," whispered the Syndicate in the ear of a harassed Premier, "it would be unjust to have to pay you income tax on what you have to pay us."

The "syndicate" idea began to appeal to the Governments of the other States, which were now all Labor ruled. The fact that the British Government had taken over private factories and distributed all profits over 10 per cent., gave Socialism such an advertisement that before the war had ended, Queensland and Victoria had joined the other Australian States and declared for Labor.

The Syndicate idea appealed to Labor Governments.

It seemed an easy way to get rid of responsibility. Of course, the time would come when the bill would have to be paid—but that was a matter posterity would have to look at—and besides, as one Minister blatantly shouted: "What has posterity done for us?"

CHAPTER XXVII.

The Rise of the "Syndicate."

The failure of the Australian manufacturers' campaign had its ludicrous side.

Prior to the termination of the war, all their talk was based upon these war-cries—"German manufacturers must be wiped off the earth." "Kill German trade and you kill their capacity for mischief." "Smash Germany now for all time." So "Trade only with the Empire and its brave Allies."

It was noticeable what fraternal consideration the manufacturers gave "the brave Allies."

As they put it ... "Those brave brothers of freedom are fighting shoulder to shoulder with the sons of the Empire, mingling their blood upon the fields of Europe in the battle for the world's civilisation."

So the "Brave Allies" were mentioned on every pamphlet issued during the war.

Of course, there were a few oversights regarding the Allies.

For instance, in an exhibition of manufactured goods, only the "Australian-made" were given any prominence. There may have been some "made by the brave Allies," but they were not very conspicuous.

It was also an oversight forgetting the "Brave Allies" when the U.S.A., taking the occasion of the stoppage of trade with Europe, joined hands with the Australian Governments in encouraging trade across the Pacific.

But the "Brave Allies" were mentioned in all the after dinner speeches—till the end of the war.

Then came a change. The manufacturers dropped their cloak of hypocrisy and made a straight-out appeal—"Only Buy Goods Made in Australia." The "Brave Allies" were dropped. Heavy duties were requested on all imported goods, whether they were made in Britain, Belgium, Bagdad or Beloochistan.

But the manufacturers were too late. They should have played that trump-card nine months before. Their first duty should have been to Australia. Their battle-cries from the beginning should have been—"Australia First"; and: "By being true to ourselves we can best contribute to Empire solidarity"; also: "The increased strength of the units will mean the more powerful whole."

Then the soldiers began to return from Europe. They found the same trouble their comrades were meeting in England, most of the jobs they had left had disappeared.

Many of the employers who had loudly boasted that the jobs of those who enlisted would be kept waiting for them, had done practically nothing to keep their promise.

During the war, when they should have been busy keeping the wheels moving, they had lost confidence.

They had forgotten that the times called for the best in every man and woman; that the first duty of those who could not go to the fighting line of Europe was to get in the fighting line of business at home; that full speed at home was absolutely necessary not only to keep a level of prosperity that would, at the end of the war, find the country well prepared to meet the inevitable heavy taxation, but to keep business at full strength so that when our soldiers returned they would have found places ready to be filled.

They had forgotten that slump is often only a mental attitude, and that even bad times can be bettered by putting an extra ounce into every pound of business energy. They had forgotten that if everyone made a move business would shift along at a faster pace. But they had done nothing but talk; so trade slackened generally and lack of business made many other vacant places besides those vacated by the men who went to the Front.

Australia wanted a commercial Kitchener, to get together business managers and labor leaders, and talk them into a better business output.

Instead of uniting together for the one common end to speedily end the war with credit to the Empire, politicians still kept up their bitter contentious legislation.

Instead of concentrating the whole of Australia's political machinery on the defence of the Empire and heartening the men with the knowledge of whole-souled support and sympathy, Australian Labor Governments devoted most of their attention to paltry party politics.

Instead of inviting workers to put in a little extra vim in time of stress; in fact, to be a bit more generous in their output, the labor leaders urged the workers to be more militant, to grip bad times as a fitting occasion to demand more wages and less hours. So the employers sat entrenched behind their desks, watching the political moves of the workers, as the Allies peered at the Germans across the trench edges of the Aisne—sat there till the soldiers came home and found no work to do.

There were cheers for them when they went out and they got some more when they came back, but they did not get much else. And they kept on coming back. A foolish politician blurted out: "Those unemployed soldiers are becoming a public nuisance."

The Federal Prime Minister, by whose Ministry the military forces were controlled, was in a quandary.

On one side, the manufacturers were telling him how to solve the problem.

"Put on thumping big taxes and help our factories to get busy, then we can take on the unemployed soldiers."

On the other side, the importers were advising the Prime Minister to drop the customs tariff and allow imports free. That, they explained, would cheapen the cost of living, and those out of work would have a better chance to live.

Then the "Syndicate," which had now grown to a great size, which, in fact, was controlling Government work in all the States, had a long consultation with the Prime Minister.

"Never mind the manufacturer," it said. "Remember, there are three stages in this country's development—Pastoral, Agricultural, and Manufacturing. The latter should be the last considered by Australia, which is a pastoral and agricultural country. We can develop Australia as it should be developed, by constructing irrigation schemes and opening agricultural areas. We could solve your unemployed problem, give your soldiers a good living wage and increase your country's prosperity. All we ask is that the Federal Government follow the States' example, and pay us 10 per cent. on the first five years expenditure, the whole amount of which we shall return at the end of that period with five per cent. added, provided you arrange with the States to give us, free of taxation, land they do not require."

A hurried conference of State Premiers was called and the situation was carefully studied. Unemployed were crowding Australian cities. Private enterprise was being crippled by the heavy income taxes imposed by State Governments to pay the increasing cost of the "Syndicates" controlling the Public Works of the various States. It was admitted that these works were being efficiently carried out, and being mostly railway and developmental constructions, they would be productive when completed. Still, with private enterprise choked off, investment was at a low level. The manufacturer was also being hard hit, for although some of the tariff duties imposed by the Federal Government helped him, each State appointed a Necessary Commodities Commission to regulate prices. The manufacturer, who was being helped by the tariff, had to pay high wages to manufacture his goods, but the Commodities Commission prevented him raising his prices so that he could not sell at a profitable figure. He, therefore, shut down and threw another mob of unemployed on the market.

Another factor that affected the matter was the great flow of immigration forwarded to Australia from Europe.

The Great War had put a sort of terror into the souls of men, and the fear of heavy taxation that threatened to follow drove them across the seas.

Every boat carried its full complement; so that when the "Syndicate" declared its intention to open up agricultural areas, each State recognised that this would not only absorb the unemployed, but as land development meant development in other quarters, a general prosperity would naturally follow. Hence they vied with each other in offering free of charge the choicest Crown lands.

The States recognised that the Crown lands had cost them nothing, and that the Commonwealth, having control of customs and land taxation, could easily raise the money for the cost of developing them.

So the "Syndicate" idea began to develop, and many capitalists who were being driven out of Europe by the uprising of Socialism, came to Australia and quietly invested in the "Syndicate" until the world saw the anomaly of a Socialistic country having all its public works and great armies of workers under the control of a capitalistic syndicate, which was now getting the opportunity to extend its scope of action by being offered tax-free land areas!

———

I will not soon forget the joy of having that letter from Australia. It was the second I had received since the Great War began.

I read it to Helen in a pretty little house which was perched upon the cliff above the Meuse, at Dinant, and which was our honeymoon home. Madame had come in to spend some days with us, and as I read the letter before the glowing fire, for it was in the winter of 1916, I could see her eyes sparkle with interest.

———

CHAPTER XXVIII.

The Age of Brain Passes.

The war was a blessing to Germany. In cutting out the old military system it gave wider opportunity for manufacturing. Young men, instead of spending their days in military training, went into business, and things boomed.

The war had caused a great outcry against German-made goods, yet when peace came and dropped the barriers, the manufactures of Germany began to flood the world.

Germany's indemnity of £1,000,000,000 could only be paid from its manufactures, so the Allied nations took every opportunity to see that those goods got into circulation.

Though British, Russian and French merchants during the war had tried to "kill German trade," as money was urgently required the Allies had to let it live, and see that it had a vigorous life in order to get their indemnity without delay. That was why Australia, as well as other parts of the British Empire, was advised to lift tariff restrictions on German goods. It was an extraordinary request, and later on was to have a world-wide effect.

I remembered a remark Nap once made to me during one of our yarns whilst waiting behind the fighting lines on the Aisne for the dawn to call us into the air.

"It's blamed hard," he said, "to have this war in our life time. It's going to throw the world back thirty years, and thirty years in a fellow's life is a mighty big hunk. This war had to come. The world had been moving too quickly during the last ten years, which saw wireless, flying, radium, and other marvellous stunts—in fact, the world had rushed ahead so swiftly that it had to pull up to take breath. This war is giving the earth breathing space, but it's going to take thirty years to clear up the mess, wipe the stains away and patch mankind up physically and mentally."

But time proved that Nap, like all the other gloomy prophets of bad times, was wrong. The war speeded up things. Men, flushed with the activity of the battlefield, came back quick-witted. Country louts and city boys, who had been taken in hand and trained to physical perfection for the battlefield, came back in twelve months—men.

There was prosperity everywhere. All Western Europe, with the exception of Belgium had declared for Socialism. The Humanist (Socialist) trend of things made high wages for the workers everywhere. But the capitalists were being hit hard. Their factory profits were dwindling away under Humanist rule, and as each one went under, the Government would take over his business. Great estates were taxed and super-taxed, till the owners had to relinquish them.

The Socialistic ideal of "all sharing the wealth of the wealthy" was rapidly approaching, but bringing with it a social cataclysm.

There was no doubt of that. It was being hastened by the lessened output of the workers. The ca-canny system ruled everywhere. With good pay for little work there was no incentive to excel, and from "little work" to "no work" was an easy step for many, as under the Humanist rule the unemployed were also paid.

The people were rapidly losing self-respect. With their false idea of equality, discipline was difficult to maintain, and lawlessness was rife.

People were so sick of war that in most of the nations disarmament was an easy matter. Even the German Navy, that was passed over to the Allied nations at the termination of the war rapidly deteriorated from lack of discipline and reduced votes for upkeep.

War was looked upon as a waste of blood and a waste of heroism, so the manufacture of arms was declared to be illegal.

Invention practically ceased.

There was no incentive to invest, as the Humanists had gradually taxed the capitalist out of existence; and it is interesting to note how time proved that the capitalist was essential to inventive progress.

The State desired to improve the flying machine, as flying was still confined to the aeroplane and the dirigible.

The then type of aeroplane could not rise or descend vertically, and only kept in the air when at great speed. The dirigible balloon was of the Zeppelin type, and was not always dependable.

It was decided to invent a machine that could easily rise and descend, and could rest in the air and be independent of all atmospheric conditions. So a State flying machine factory was commenced in England on Salisbury Plain.

The first trouble arose when the building was being erected. Many workers objected to what was called the waste of labor. It was pointed out that under the Socialistic rule, the product of labor had to go to labor, and as the building of the flying machine factory was not producing food or clothing, and the workers on it had to be supported by the labor of the whole community, it was making a distinct class of them, which was illegal. However, the Government went on with the work.

The first machine made was not successful. Then an agitation ensued that it was not equitable and just that the community should support any labor engaged in such a foolish enterprise. It was demanded that the factory should be closed, and the workers set at useful employment, instead of being a burden on the state and reviving the old system of classes.

I remember reading at the time that a leader in the experiments named Cooley, pointed out that the successful machine would save much labor in after years, by giving more efficient means of transport, and that when the successful machine was built the whole community would enjoy the result of the labor expended on it.

"The First Wright Aeroplane."

He pointed out that in the production of the first aeroplane, the Wright Brothers had spent years of effort in the solution of the problem of aerial navigation, and that a vast amount of labor and material was consumed before the first practical machine was made, so it was, therefore, reasonable to consider that much expenditure of labor and material would have to continue till the perfect machine was found, and that it was worth it all to win that ideal means of transport. The labor of the hand and brain to achieve the perfect flying machine would have to be directed either by a capitalist or by the State. There were now no capitalists, and it was, therefore, the duty of the State to take the matter up notwithstanding the so-called waste of labor and material.

He pointed out that all industry involved waste. That millions of pounds had been spent in experiments in evolving the machines we were using to-day. He also mentioned that he remembered, when in America, that millions of dollars were spent in attempting to tunnel under the Hudson River, at New York, and that many failures were met with before the work was successfully achieved.

He might also have mentioned that all this expense was borne by the capitalist, and that if the State had had charge of it, the enormous waste of money in experiments would have caused a public panic.

He pleaded that all great inventions were developed on expensive experimenting, and the perfect flying machine could only be won in the same way.

The State flying machine factory was, therefore, given another opportunity, and the second flying machine was made. On its first test it failed to rise, so the public objected to the mad enterprise and refused to support the experiments in unprofitable labor. The factory was closed, and the workers put at employment that "showed results."

I mention this incident of the flying machine, as the same opposition was met in other branches of science.

Thus the spirit of invention was suppressed. There was no anxiety to achieve, no desire for individual excellence. With invention ceasing the Age of Brain went out—that Age of Brain that brilliant period in the world's history which only covered one hundred years, yet saw the rise and development of the most brilliant scientists the world had ever seen!

Great brains rose in one brief space of a century, and gave the world railways, steam navigation, electric telegraphs, the telephone, gas and electric lighting, photography, the phonograph, the X-Ray, spectrum analysis, anæsthetics, antiseptics, radium, the cinematograph, the automobile, wireless telegraphy, and the aeroplane; all perfectly new departures from anything previously devised!

That wonderful Age of Brain passed out, giving place to the Age of Brawn!

It was the sunset of ambition, and the remarkable events that followed are all so recent that to give details seems like telling news of general knowledge.

CHAPTER XXIX.

The Trumpet Blast.

It will be remembered that, at the close of the European War, the allied nations of Western Europe had requested Canada, India, Australia, and Africa to open their ports to free admission of German-made goods. Those colonies at first demurred, but assented and gradually drifted towards independence.

During the war these colonies had sent their contingents to help the Mother Country, and at the declaration of peace desired an Imperial Federation throughout the British Empire, but the politicians in the Humanist Government saw no profit in Empire connections. Sentiment had no place in Socialistic policies.

Canada gave free trade to the United States of America, and the barriers between India and the surrounding nations were dropped, whilst the various parts of the British Empire gradually drew apart from Great Britain.

In Asia, freedom of exchange between the nations had welded Russia, India, China, Japan and Siam into a great federation of wonderful prosperity. It was called "the United Nations of Asia."

The barriers of trade that formerly existed between these nations seemed as absurd as a farmer dividing his farm into little plots and trying to cultivate all kinds of plants on each plot instead of putting only wheat in wheat land and corn in corn land.

As Owasi, the great Japanese statesman who brought about the coalition, put it, "Let Asia have the intelligence to utilise its lands to the best advantage. Let it develop each nation's products as the result of natural selection. We can grow rice in India, we can grow wheat in Russia. We can put up a high tariff wall and grow rice in Russia, if we grow it in a hothouse; but it would not be so profitable as raising wheat. Tariff walls are trade restrictions. They are as obsolete as the great wall of China."

"But freedom of exchange will close up some industries," said a critic.

"Yes, if they are run at a loss," Owasi replied, "and besides, some one must pay for that loss, and a loss to one nation instantly acts upon others. Freedom of interchange of trade is reciprocal, both nations gain or they wouldn't trade —and there is amity. When trade is restrained competition commences. Competition soon becomes jealous of the restricted territory and war begins. Commercial wars often begin with a tariff and end with a shell. It is at first a commercial war, but as its intensity develops the bullet and the shell come in.

Artificial barriers are obsolete in these days of flying. The airship should be the peace-bringer of the world."

So Eastern and Central Asia developed into great producing nations with the consequent desire for trade expansion—particularly with Australia and with the markets of Western Europe.

The great Asiatic federation opened up close trade relations with Australia. This movement, strange to say, had been predicted in Sydney as far back as April, 1915, when at a public reception to some Japanese journalists, it was pointed out that a most serious moment in the history of Australia would occur when the Australian came back from the big job in Europe, that when he had put his gun in the corner and had taken off his coat for business, he would see the rapidly developing nations of Eastern Asia about to dominate the Pacific trade, and that he would then be wise if he decided at the outset to formulate a policy of peaceful progress and preserve the closest and most friendly trade relations with Japan and Eastern Asia.

Australia, therefore, joined in a trade treaty with Eastern Asia, but Western Europe refused.

It considered that the flooding of its markets with cheap-made Asiatic goods would mean serious opposition to home factories, which were being run under high wages.

Belgium alone stood for freedom of trade exchange with Asia. This single nation in Western Europe that had stood against Socialism was now a nation of great manufacturing capacity, a country of wealthy people, a haven for the thoughtful and the ambitious who were forced out of Humanist nations. Belgium was the centre of European invention.

It could foresee trouble in restricting Asiatic desires for trade exchange, and pleaded with the nations of Western Europe to open their ports. It was pointed out, that out of 300 of the wars in the history of the world, 272 were due to trade causes and only 28 were due to religious or other causes.

It was pointed out that freedom of trade between German States had made Germany so strong, that in 1914 it could fight a fifteen months war with the greatest nations of the world.

But the Humanist nations, being non-militant, turned a deaf ear.

Then a threat of war came from Asia!

It came like a trumpet blast in the ear of a sleeping man, and it found Western Europe unprepared—with its energy wasted under the rule of Socialism, and with its armies and navies almost deteriorated out of existence.

CHAPTER XXX.

Wilbrid Passes Out.

I remember it was the afternoon of Christmas Day, 1916.

Madame had come across to our little home at Dinant for a few days' rest.

She had almost worked herself to sickness in her active campaign of organising in preparation for the war-storm that threatened Europe.

We were sitting on the verandah, overlooking the river, when we noticed far down the zig-zag track that led to the house, a black-cloaked figure. It was coming towards us and walked with the aid of a stick. As it approached, it brought to my memory a similar figure I had met on the Coblenz road; and I told Madame the story of my meeting with Wilbrid.

"If that is Wilbrid," she exclaimed, "he is spying. He must not see me here."

I explained that it could not be the Great Humanist, as, eighteen months before, he had changed his clerical garb for that of a civilian; and this figure was old and bent, whereas Wilbrid was tall and erect.

I then went down the track to investigate. Within a hundred yards, the person stopped and raised his hand.

"Jefson," was all he said.

It was Wilbrid!—but old, careworn, and almost out of breath.

"Why this change?" I asked, as I came up to him and we moved to a seat at the side of the track.

"I'm down and out," he said. "My mission failed." And his chin sank upon the top of the hand-clasped stick. "The crowd did not understand. You know that I began to preach the doctrine of the Humanist to help the masses to come into their own. You know we won upon the wave of reaction that followed the war. We should have stayed at that level and moved along, but the momentum was too great, the pendulum had swung too far; for when the masses ruled they sinned worse than the party they supplanted. They became more bitter autocrats than the rulers we suppressed.

"Instead of 'Justice for the People,' it was 'Brute Strength for the Mob.'

"I could not stem the flood that I had let loose. Heaven only knows how hard I tried, for when I pleaded that a moderate track be taken, the mob insisted that I sought a place to dominate, and put me in the rut.

"To-day they fear no law of man or God. To-day their self-satisfaction has made them indifferent to anything that elevates. I had led them into a morass, and deeper in the mire have they rushed!"

He sat silent and watched the shadows creeping along the river.

"And what now?" I asked.

"I am going back—back to the monastery. I misread the world, I misread human nature. I was one of the fools who think they know all the statesmanship that controls the destinies of nations, who think their petty untrained minds can grasp the great problems of diplomacy.

"I have found you can only qualify for high administrative posts by unselfish study. You cannot create a statesman by the mere toss of a coin at a political meeting. Though people fitted to rule and lead men to build mighty nations are sometimes born in obscurity, they cannot develop there.

"But I meant rightly—I meant rightly. In my ignorance I have played with a sharp-edged weapon, and it is turning upon me and—civilisation."

"How?" I queried.

"A cataclysm is coming," he said. "I can feel it. No, it will not be within Asia, as many people fear, but within Europe.

"The hasty structure of Humanism cannot stand. Even now it is toppling. It is going to crash, and from the ruins another creed will rise, a creed, I trust, more rational.

"I was passing home, so came to tell you."

Then Madame came down the track.

Wilbrid rose as she approached. His hand shook as he removed his black broad-brimmed hat. They stood before each other for a moment without a word.

For the first time, these leaders faced each other. Then Wilbrid bent his head.

"You have won," he said. "You have won."

"It took you some time to find that out," she remarked, with a trembling voice. "I could have told you that soon after you began. You cried for the destruction of the very things that have made the world progress. You aimed to destroy individuality and you did so—but only with your own class.

"You have preached that all wealth is the result of labor, but now you have realised that intelligent supervision is required to make labor effective, and that brains are just as necessary to the world's prosperity as is manual toil.

"You went out to reform society and level down; and your party no sooner won some power than your women-folk tried to form a "social set" of their own— you don't know women. You are as ignorant of their desires as you are of your own. You do not know it is woman's instinct to be something more than a drab. There is more of the divine spark in the woman than in the man. It should be so with the producers of men. She yearns for uplift, even if it be the sneered-at "society" you sought to crush.

"You have only to note how, when Socialist politicians in any country win any power, their wives crowd each other into those circles of society, that husbands had won notoriety by attacking as "loafing on the workers.""

"You have only to note the social columns of the daily press of those countries to see how anxious these wives of Socialist members are to have their names in print that they have had "afternoon-tea" with ladies of any title.

"Deep in the heart of every woman is respect for the title or the decorative side of human life. A flower to her is something more than a thing.

"You women will tell you you do not know them—and how could you?— you, a man who lived the greater part of your life in a monastery apart from your fellows, apart from the problems, apart from the battle against conditions that make men—men. You, in the seclusion of your own kind, conceived dreams of Utopian madness and you came forth and cast your foolish fancies like a net upon the ignorant. And now you find your failings; you see the petty smallness of your ideals and you retreat—back into your abbey like a frightened crab creeping beneath the cover of a stone."

"I know it now," said the crestfallen man. "We can only learn our lessons through bitter experience."

He turned upon his heel as if to leave.

She was touched by the pathetic figure and held out her hand to him.

He took it in his and bent over it.

"Good-bye," he said. "I go home on this day of days, this day of 'peace on earth and good will to men'—and alas! the world a seething mass of discontent!"

I brought him to the house and gave him some wine to drink.

"Good-bye," he said. "God bless you." And he waved his hat as we watched the careworn figure slowly stroll down the track and pass out of our lives.

CHAPTER XXXI.

The Wonderful Month of War.

Then the great war crashed upon Europe, and it did not come from Asia!

Its sudden outbreak proved many things; first, that invention had not been entirely exterminated; and second, that artificial laws could not destroy the divine in humanity.

Above all, the war proved that brawn could not suppress the aspiring flights of the brain; for during the socialistic era of "human equality," men with more highly developed inventive faculties, men who wished to cultivate the spirit that inspires the human to ever excel, met in mysterious places and plotted!

They felt the time must eventually arrive when the unnatural social position the Humanists adopted must overbalance itself; hence they prepared for the impending cataclysm.

It is strange, in the history of the world, how a thread of sympathy mysteriously binds together those whose souls are suffering from a common tyranny.

Throughout Europe bands of scientific militants of both sexes met in secret conclave and plotted for "Another Day."

Yet the great secrecy observed by these insurgents was unnecessary. The Humanist policy of non-considering and non-observing, of suppressing originality of thought as being useless in an age of equality, had dulled the thinking faculty in its followers. Nature has no use for the non-used, so the socialists were developing into living and working human automata, in fact, taking life more like an advanced kind of animal. Was it, therefore, any wonder that they were blind to the developing danger?

The same circumstances quickened the inventive faculty of the oppressed. Danger quickens intuition, and the spark of invention shone brightly in many covert places.

Thought was, however, concentrated on one object, the quickest and surest method of overthrowing the Humanist policy and installing an ideal method of living in which not only would there be "equal opportunities for all," which, though it was the policy of the Humanists at their inauguration, had developed into "equal opportunities for leaders," but there would also be the rule of "payment by results."

Inventive genius concentrated upon two objectives:—First, an ideal method of secret communication between followers; and second, the most efficient fighting machine—a weapon that would only require a minimum of personnel to operate. With such a weapon, a small force, such as the Individualists numbered, would be a match for a multitude.

The ideal means of inter-communication was invented by a Belgian. It was simply the improvement of the method of transmitting and receiving a certain type of ether wave through the earth. This wave did not need aerials, and could only be received and transmitted through certain instruments that were kept in sacred seclusion in secret places.

With these instruments followers were ever in close touch with each other, and co-operative measures were detailed for the day of general uprising.

The fighting machine was also invented by a Belgian. It was the ideal flying machine, sought since the Wright Brothers conquered the air ten years before.

The old style of aeroplane only kept in the air when at a great speed, hence it could not hover. As a weapon of offence it had, therefore, many disadvantages in bomb-dropping or other belligerent action. These disadvantages increased according to the height from which the aeroplane would have to operate; and as the German War of 1915 had improved the range of air cannon, the old type aeroplane was almost useless for offence purposes. The dirigible balloon, being lighter than air, was not always dependable, and having also to operate from a great height, the rarefied air in those regions seriously affected the gas carriers.

The Belgian "Heliocoptre" carried its propellers above the machine; the axles, having "universal" joints, enabled them to revolve in any plane, whilst engines, operating by means of powerful, non-clogging explosives, generated the enormous power. These "Heliocoptres" were armed with great "Thermit" shells, which, when they struck and burst, would not only set free a paralysing gas, but would also produce a molten "thermit" mass of a heat of over 5000 degrees, which could burn its way even through armored plate.

It is too recent for me to detail, at length, the remarkable circumstances following the prescribed day, when these machines simultaneously rose in various cities, and after but a week's reign of terror took possession of all Governments in the Humanist nations.

The people generally were not antagonistic to a change of rule. They were tired of the unnatural life and almost listlessly waited developments. These did not tarry, for within a very short period the present systems of Commission Governments were adopted, and Royalties were recalled to their various kingdoms as governing figureheads.

I only briefly mention this, the shortest war in history, because it was so recent. Yet it had the greatest bearing upon human development.

Belgium came through it untouched, though it held the centre of operations.

I shall never forget that wonderful month of war, and the almost superhuman energy Madame displayed in assisting to direct operations. It was not strange that her constitution collapsed under the remarkable strain, and that for a while death hovered round the sick room. Her complete recovery called for a long sea voyage, which explained why we entered Sydney Harbor some weeks later.

CHAPTER XXXII.

What Happened in Australia.

I found Australia in a strange way.

Every State had a "socialistic" Government, and yet all public works were controlled by combines of capitalists. The business interests of these combines were so interlocked as to be one huge concern generally known as the "Syndicate." It carried out all constructional works at a percentage on the cost. The percentage and interest on the capital invested were raised by the Commonwealth and State Governments mainly from customs duties at first and, when these slackened, as they did later, from land taxation.

It seemed strange to find that the Socialist Governments had actually handed over the Australian States to the oft'-maligned capitalist; and, stranger still, the people did not complain. The fact of the matter was that the people had found that socialistic theories were very fine for platform platitudes, but not for practical politics.

Australia learnt over again the lesson she should have remembered from an experiment of twenty years previously.

It was the old story of "New Australia": the story that taught the world that ideal socialism is impossible whilst human nature is as it is. And yet Australia had forgotten it! It is strange that people rarely profit from past failures. Countries as well as peoples usually insist on buying their own experience, and the history of the socialistic experiment in Australia between 1910 and 1917 was simply a repetition of the great failure of William Lane's ideal.

It is interesting, at this stage, to study the analogy.

In 1890, a brilliant-phrasing Socialist, named William Lane, set Queensland workers' minds aflame with his Utopian dreams of the ideal socialistic life that could be lived on a large tract of country offered them in the heart of South America. Three years later 250 Australians, including 60 single men and many single girls, put all their wealth into a common fund and sailed away from Australia in a specially chartered ship.

It was a unique experiment in Socialism. The men were not the scum of cities, but enthusiastic and hearty individuals; clean-thinking Irishmen, for the most part, trained in the tasks of settlement. All were equal, and the warmest comradeship existed between men and women.

Here was the first weakness of the Socialistic creed: by all contributing to a common fund, Lane had provided for communism of goods; by recognising all children as belonging to the State he had provided for communism of children; but as a father and a husband he feared communism of morals. Hence he framed a regulation aimed to preserve the conventional relations between the sexes, especially on board ship. To prevent "flirtations" he issued a decree forbidding women to appear on deck after sunset!

The first dissension arose through the women objecting to remain in the stuffy atmosphere of the ship's hold below the water line from sunset to sunrise, and, as each woman claimed equality with Lane, the notice was torn down. Lane, however, produced a bundle of proxies from members of the movement in Australia, so that his single vote constituted a majority! He then assumed the post of dictator.

The party then split into two factions; one that believed in Lane, and the other that objected to his despotic control and questioned his right to allot to them the "dirty jobs," such as "washing up" and "scrubbing the decks."

After many trying adventures the socialists reached the site of the communistic settlement and found opportunity to study and compare Socialism in practice and in theory. They had at last done away with the bad old methods of capitalism, which "ground the people down and robbed them of rest, energy, food and life"; so the "New Australians" determined to avoid drudgery in their new life, and were very keen on being properly "uplifted." There were a number of musical instruments in the stores, so thirty-six socialists formed a band and practised assiduously in the pleasant shade of the trees for a considerable proportion of the time they should have been clearing timber and building houses under the tropical sun.

Those who toiled hardest protested, but Lane, with a stern hand and a revolver in his belt put down revolt and punished those who disputed his decision by setting them the most disagreeable tasks.

Against Lane's decision there was no appeal. Three men disobeyed him and he ordered them out of the colony. One of them had put £1000 into the venture and wanted to argue. Lane, however, called in a posse of native soldiers, armed to the teeth. They marched into the camp with fixed bayonets, and the three malcontents were taken out and cast adrift.

One of the "faithful" wrote at this time:—

"We have surrendered all civil rights and become mere cogs in a wheel. We are no longer active factors in the scheme of civilisation: in fact, each man is practically a slave. Lane does the thinking; we do the work. Result—barbarism!"

A third of the party soon broke camp and threw themselves upon the charity of Paraguay. Those who stayed behind shortly afterwards expelled Lane. With forty-five sympathisers he set out to establish another Paradise!

Those who stayed behind drew up a series of regulations that made any change a subject for universal discussion, and as the regulations were being continually altered, public gatherings took up most of the day's work. Convening meetings and arguing thereat was found much more interesting than toiling in the hot sun; so practically little work was done.

A Frenchman had a little farm close by and was making a small fortune from it for himself, whilst thirty-five Australians next to him could not make a living for each other! So much for the advantages of Socialistic co-operation!

Soon the "New Australians" had to get busy to prevent starvation. One of the many authoritative writers said:—

> A brief but brilliant span of existence may be attained by a Socialistic State living on the capital of its predecessors, but it soon runs through the capital and goes out like a spent squib and leaves a nasty smell.

(New South Wales also found this out ten years later.)

Instead of the "New Australians" getting busy and making the profits that awaited the exploitation of the wonderful timber on their area, they looked for easy work and fancied they found it in the cultivation of ramie fibre.

The fibre failed; money was being exhausted; the leaders were faced with two propositions. They had either to set the people at productive labor, such as timber-getting, or raise money somehow, somewhere. They followed the latter as being the easier task. So they sold to an outside capitalist the exclusive right for three years of cutting timber on the area. They sold it for an absurdly small consideration, to find later that they were also prevented cutting wood for their own uses!

Although Lane had started a new colony, he made but two innovations. He ruled that as woman's only sphere was in the home, he would abolish the woman's vote. His other innovation for an ideal Socialist community was the employment of cheap native labor. He thus revived the "wicked capitalistic idea of cheap—nigger labor."

It was also found that the inclusion of the native element had a serious effect upon the morality of the Socialists. There was a remarkable increase of half-caste children without the formality of marriage with the Paraguayians.

Communism was still advocated, yet to the communistic dining table each man brought his private bottle of treacle, which he stowed away between meals under his pillow or in some other secret hiding place. Children grew up godless and ignorant and—Lane disappeared!

The original population was reduced to 22 men, 17 women and 51 children.

It was decided to abandon Socialism and let each man work for himself instead of "each for all and all for each." Then things began to prosper. The ambition of each was to become a capitalist. There was no talk of an "eight- hour day"! From sunrise to sunset men, women, and children worked, and in an incredibly short time houses rose, gardens developed and later teachers came to uplift the children and to start a Sunday School.

What is left of "New Australia" to-day is an average community of sane, sober and hard-working farmers, taking as their motto: "What we have, we hold"!

Yet the failure of that experiment was forgotten in the rush of Socialistic legislation that gripped Australia before and during the war; and the rise of the "Syndicate" saved Australia from a similar wreck that followed the previous experiment.

The "Syndicate" idea began to develop. It became another name for co-operation. The keen people at the head of it saw that its continued success depended on the people having an interest in the profits of their work, so they gave the public opportunity to share in it.

The "Syndicate" expanded its sphere of co-operation. Did a State factory fail, then, if there was a chance of profit in the material it manufactured, a co-operation "Syndicate"—a subsidiary branch of the combine—took it over. The workers, supplanted by labor-saving machinery, were taken up by the great farms the "Syndicate" was developing throughout the country.

The "Syndicate," however, did not encourage manufacture unless the goods could be made cheaper and better than they could be imported duty free. It studied every new manufacturing proposition apart from any tariff possibilities. The first point it considered was whether it was advisable to establish in Australia a factory with necessarily expensive power to compete with Canadian or other factories that utilised cheap water power.

This policy naturally brought about two conditions. It established manufacture on an honest basis by doing away with the necessity for the usual political wire-pulling for the imposition of tariff duties, and it gradually brought about free trade in goods not worth manufacturing in Australia.

From an industrial point of view the "Syndicate" system revolutionised the lot of the Australian worker. It fixed a minimum wage, much higher than the then ruling rate, and instituted piece-work. The regular wage was guaranteed whatever the output, and the piece-work rate was added to it.

The "Syndicate" introduced scientific management and, from a business point of view, considered men first and profits second. It knew that better working conditions resulted in easier and more profitable work. It considered the conditions of labor by grading employees. It studied their equipment and noted if tools, benches or machines were best fitted for the people who used them. It saw that a "five-foot" man was not given a "six-foot" shovel, or that a short girl-worker was not sitting on a seat that would be more comfortable for a tall girl. It fitted the equipment to the worker just as a shoe is fitted to the foot.

It studied the work as well as the equipment. Each part of the work was specially arranged to eliminate unnecessary movements until it became so standardised as to give the worker the easiest way of doing it properly. Working hours were shortened; yet more work was done. Each worker did what he could do best. Profit-sharing was introduced in all ventures, but it was based upon individual effort; in fact, the "Syndicate" combine was a system of organisation and profitable co-operation, a system that put the Socialist out of business.

Organisation and co-operation stopped the mad war upon private enterprise and industry. It found the value of men lay in their ability to think individually and act collectively. Trade Unionism did not do that. It is true it helped the workman to secure higher wages, better working conditions and shorter hours, but it was not satisfied with that. It sought absolute ownership of factories and all means of production, with evasion of responsibilities and no provision made against deficits.

The Trade Unionist called for opportunity for all, but denied it to those workers who could not afford to pay the entrance fee to the union.

Whilst the Trade Unionist, on the one hand, was getting highest wages from private enterprise, on the other hand, he demanded from the State cheap house rentals—as at Daceyville and other State-controlled suburbs.

The Australian worker, therefore, practically lived upon Government charity, until the Government was beggared and the capitalist "Syndicate" providentially stepped in and saved the country.

It was well for Australia that the capitalists considered the individual, and that it was just as good business to have efficient machinists as well as efficient machines.

It was well for Australia that the capitalists knew the value of human flesh and nurtured it. And Australia understood. In the stress of the German War it had sobered up. It had dropped the Utopian dreams of the impracticable and used its head. It saw an analogy in the system of the "Syndicate," "Organisation and Co-operation," to a similar system that had led them to victory on the battlefields of Europe.

The perfect organisation that military training gave, and the intense co-operation the call of the blood demanded, instilled these two great principles into Australian character.

The great German War was worth while to Australia.

It is evening as I write these concluding phrases. I look across Sydney Harbor from my Cremorne home, and I see the city skyline edged with a glistening fringe.

Beyond the distant hills of purple blue the sun is sinking in a saffron sky.

Into the evening air the homeward 'planes are rising from the city park.

A faint report comes from the sunset gun and starts a train of vision running through my mind.

I hear again the gun that brought me from the sky into the Forest of the Argonne, and then "Nap" passes through my thoughts. (He is now in charge of a Syndicate concern.)

Madame then comes into vision. (She is now the "gran'ma" of my home.)

Then Wilbrid totters across my field of thought.

And then Helen—but my reverie has ended....

She calls me in.

(The End.)